The Winds of Catawba

Laurie Stahl

THOMAS NELSON PUBLISHERS
Nashville • Atlanta • London • Vancouver

Published in Nashville, Tennessee, by Thomas Nelson, Inc., Publishers, and distributed in Canada by Word Communications, Ltd., Richmond, British Columbia, and in the United Kingdom by Word (UK), Ltd., Milton Keynes, England.

Library of Congress Cataloging-in Publication Data

Stahl, Laurie.

The winds of Catawba / Laurie Stahl.

p. cm.

"Sequel to The women of Catawba."

ISBN 0-8407-5081-1 (pbk.)

1. Charleston (S.C.)—History—1775-1865—Fiction. I. Title.

PS3569.T312W56 1995

813'.54—dc20 94-37439

CIP

Printed in the United States of America

2 3 4 5 6 7 - 01 00 99 98 97 96 95

In Loving memory of
my mother, Hilda Stahl
I miss you, Mom!

Laurel Marston was growing impatient. It was late afternoon and the Marston women—Maida, Taylor, Kendra, and Laurel—sat in the downstairs parlor enjoying their afternoon tea. Moments ago the mail had been delivered with a letter for Laurel from her friend Clair Portland back in England and, not wanting to read it in front of the others, she was saving it for later. The conversation between Maida and Taylor Marston faded into the background as Laurel anticipated her reading.

First she would have to make sure Kendra, her sister, wouldn't interrupt. She would go up to her bedroom and place a chair near the window or maybe sit out on the balcony. She would arrange herself comfortably and gracefully as befitting a young lady. And then, Laurel would read every single word that Clair had written.

No one watching Laurel would have guessed at the excitement bursting inside her. But they would have noticed her beauty. The nineteen-year-old with long blonde hair, blue eyes, and a slender figure hadn't gone unnoticed by the young men in the area. She prided herself on her looks and manners. Yet, as the men continued to gather around her, she held herself apart. She had no interest in any of them. There was only one man for Laurel—Jason Portland, Clair's brother.

Laurel impatiently pulled her thoughts back to the present and waited until she could escape. When afternoon tea was over, she excused herself and ascended the stairs to her room.

A dressing table and wardrobe lined the wall nearest her door. Across the room, a poster bed reached halfway to the high ceiling, and on the wall next to the bed was a fireplace. Even though the winters weren't bad in South Carolina, there were nights when Laurel was grateful for its warmth. In front of the fireplace was the chair in which Laurel planned to read her letter.

Taking the chair out to the balcony, she sat down and opened the note.

May 21, 1802

Dearest Laurel:

I hope this letter finds you and your family well.

As for me, I can't complain. The weather here in England is dreadful. I wonder if I'll ever see the sun again. After the harsh winter we were glad for the rain, but now it doesn't look to stop. I pray daily for a ray of sunshine.

I don't wish to go on and on about such dreary things. I have wonderful news. Do you remember my brother, Jason?

Hugging the letter close, Laurel rolled her eyes heavenward. Did she remember Jason? How could she forget him?

He was the reason she hadn't wanted to leave England more than two years ago. She had begged her father to let her stay, but Yates Marston had refused.

Letters from Clair had been scarce, but each one was like a precious jewel to Laurel—even more so if Jason was mentioned. In her dreams she could see herself walking down the aisle toward the handsome Jason Portland to live happily ever after.

> *I have begged him to allow me to come to America for a visit, and he has finally given me permission! That is the reason for this letter. We will be leaving on June twelfth and arriving in your Charleston around mid-August.*

Clair was coming to Catawba! *Today is July sixteenth,* Laurel realized. *She will be here next month.* Laurel didn't know if she should be excited or nervous. Coming to Catawba had made a change in the demure lady of culture she had been in England. In the past two years she had learned to hunt, ride, and do household chores. Those were tasks that wouldn't be acceptable for a young lady in England.

Sitting back in her chair, Laurel recalled her arrival at Catawba. She had been spoiled rotten then, refusing to lift a finger around the plantation. They hadn't had all the slaves and indentured servants they had now. At that time everyone had had to pull his or her own weight.

One day Laurel had ordered an old black man, Pickle, to fetch her some honey. It had been close to sunset, and he had suggested that she wait until the next day.

"I most certainly will not wait until tomorrow," Laurel had snapped. "You will do as I say without question, or I will see that you are whipped. Do you understand me?" She had spoken in her haughtiest voice.

"Yes, Missy Laurel," Pickle relented.

No one had noticed Pickle missing until after dark. The men had organized a search. Court Yardley had been the one to find Pickle covered with bee stings, his entire body swollen and feverish. Ward Marston, Laurel's uncle, had demanded that Laurel take care of Pickle since she was responsible for his injuries.

Yet, in spite of everything, Pickle had been kind to Laurel. He had taken time to talk with her about her hatred of South Carolina. He had shown her that there were things to love in the lands around the plantation. And after he recovered, he had begun to teach Laurel how to shoot a flintlock rifle.

"I don't never want anything to happen to you, Missy Laurel. I want you to know how to shoot if you ever have to protect yourself or Catawba," Pickle had said.

Pickle and Laurel had become a common sight around Catawba. It had been so gradual that no one thought anything of it. But now that Clair Portland was coming, Laurel wondered if she would have to stop spending time with the old man. She knew it wasn't acceptable behavior for a proper lady. She went back to her letter.

The date of our arrival will depend upon the weather of course. Jason plans to dispatch a messenger upon our landing to give you ample notice of our arrival.

I hope this meets with your approval as there is no time to wait for your reply. By the time you receive this letter we will already be on board the ship sailing for your America.

Jason has just reminded me to mention that he will be accompanying me as chaperon. He is looking forward to this trip as much as I.

Please give your family our greetings and hopes they are in good health.

Your Friend,
Clair Portland

He was coming! Her Jason was finally coming to claim her as his bride. Laurel's dream was finally coming true. "Thank you, Lord, for answering my prayers," she whispered.

Clutching the letter against her breast, Laurel closed her eyes and counted slowly to ten. She was bursting with excitement, but she was determined to control her emotions. Jason would expect Laurel to act the proper lady as she had been in England.

The echo of an ax against a tree brought her back to the present. She looked out over the plantation. Old Musket was barking. People were working all over Catawba—training horses, felling trees for lumber, and preparing the fields for next year's cotton crops.

When Yates Marston had first brought his family to Catawba, their living quarters were just small cabins. Yates and his second wife, Maida, along with his three children, Laurel, Kendra, and Reid, had squeezed into one cabin.

Yates's younger brother, Ward, had married his indentured servant, Taylor, and accepted her young daughter, Brooke, into his family. Taylor had brought a runaway slave, Cammie, with her, and she also had stayed at Catawba. They had lived in a second cabin.

The house Ward had dreamed of building for his and Yates's families had been completed earlier this summer. It was a grand, three-story brick house with a porch that wrapped around the front. The second floor had a balcony that ran the length of the house, shading the porch below. Large doors opened onto the balconies and porch. The first floor housed the kitchen, dining room, parlor, offices, and Ward and Taylor's, and Brooke's rooms. The second story held bedrooms for Yates and Maida, Laurel, Kendra, and Reid, as well as several guest rooms. The top floor was for the house servants.

The small cabins the Marston families had once occupied now held slaves and bond servants. Half a dozen new outbuildings had been built around the original structures. The larger ones were for storing bales of cotton, the smaller for feed, livestock, and working equipment.

As their plantation grew, Ward and Yates had taken on more bond servants and slaves. The slaves were bought against Ward's wishes. It had been the cause of many an argument at Catawba. Yates's argument was that they would be bought anyway, so why not make sure they were treated fairly and allowed to raise their families?

So after two years, Maida and Taylor no longer had to cook and clean alone. They had slaves to do that. The gardens were taken care of by other servants, and Laurel and Kendra, who had gotten used to helping, now had little to do.

As a whole, the plantation had grown rapidly over the last two years, and Laurel had learned to love it. Now it was a thriving, industrious place. A place that Laurel could proudly show to Clair and Jason.

"Oh, Jason," Laurel whispered, "please hurry to me. I've been waiting a long time."

Kendra Marston scanned the trail anxiously. Perspiration dotted her lips and forehead. Her brown hair, damp from the heat, clung to her cheek and neck, brushing the smattering of freckles stretched across the bridge of her nose.

A slight breeze rustled the leaves on the trees, but it didn't alleviate the unbearable heat. *I wish this storm would break*, she thought. *We could do with a good rain.*

Kendra slid off her horse Turnip's back when she reached a small clearing. The riding habit she wore was suffocating. Unbuttoning the buttons of the jacket, Kendra would have removed it if her blouse underneath weren't so thin. And if Court Yardley weren't due to meet her any moment.

"Kendra."

Her eyes widened at the sight of Court. He stood with his legs slightly apart, clad in buff-colored breeches. The linen shirt that he wore was soaked with sweat, emphasizing the muscular frame beneath. His red hair, cut too short to tie back, was a riot of curls. Kendra knew there was no man as handsome as her Court.

She crossed and flung her arms around his neck. "Oh, Court, I've missed you," she murmured. His hair tickled her face as she snuggled closer.

Strong arms wrapped around Kendra's short frame, lifting her feet off the ground. Rubbing his cheek against her hair, Court groaned. Kendra smelled so clean and good. Her hair and skin reminded him of a fresh spring day.

"I've missed you too, my Kendra."

He reluctantly lowered her to the ground. Grasping her small hand in his sun-browned one, he tugged her toward a large oak tree.

"It's been ages since we've been able to spend time together," Kendra pouted.

Chuckling, Court stroked her cheek. "There's nothing we can do about it. This is a busy time for everyone. Besides, we don't want your father to become suspicious."

Her heart swelled with love. Court always had a level head when it came to their relationship. If it had been left up to Kendra, she would have informed her father of their love right away. But Court wanted to wait until he was no longer an indentured servant.

"When will you speak with my father?" she asked dreamily.

"Soon, Kendra. We have to remain patient."

"But I want my family to know how I feel about you, Court. I love you so much. If I shouted it out, people would hear me all the way to Charleston."

It was becoming more and more difficult to keep their feelings a secret. With Court's indenture coming to an end in October, it was hard not to become anxious about revealing their love to Kendra's father.

Court had tried to keep from falling in love with Kendra. When he had rescued her from a runaway barrel in Charleston, and then kissed her, he hadn't been thinking. When he discovered that she was Ward Marston's niece, he'd felt like a fool. How could he, an indentured servant, ever dream of marrying the niece of his boss?

Fighting the feelings that were churning inside him, Court hadn't counted on Kendra's determination. Everywhere he went, she was there. Trying to stay away from her had only added to his agony. In the end, Court had surrendered to his feelings and told Kendra everything. She, of course, had been overjoyed. They had decided to wait until Court would become a free man before they would tell her family. Now that the time was running out, the couple was beginning to grow anxious.

Shaking his head to clear it, Court said, "Tell me what you've been doing today. I want to hear every detail."

Kendra sighed. She understood Court's wish to change the subject. So for the next several minutes she told him everything that had happened that morning.

When Kendra finished, Court got to his feet, holding out his hand. "It's time for me to get back. I don't want anyone to miss me."

Kendra went to him. "I can't stand this, Court," she whispered. "I feel as if I'm shriveling up each time I have to leave you."

"Sssh. It'll be all right, Kendra." Rocking her back and forth like a child, Court tried to soothe her pain. He didn't want her to know that it broke his heart, too, each time they separated. He had to be strong for her. "I have something for you."

Pulling her head slightly away, Kendra looked up. "For me? What for?"

A soft chuckle rumbled in his chest. "Because I love you, and I want you to think of me every time you look at it." Reaching into the satchel strung across his shoulders, he pulled out a tiny wooden barrel.

"Oh, Court. It's beautiful." Taking it from his outstretched hand, Kendra gently ran her fingers over it. The creamy color of new oak felt smooth to her touch. Turning it around, she noticed a 'K' carved into the side. She blinked back tears and hugged it to her chest, raising her eyes to

Court. "Thank you," she whispered. "I shall think of you every time I look at it."

He couldn't help feeling proud. Court's workmanship had been sought after back in England. His father had trained him from boyhood to become a cooper. Then tragedy had struck. His father was killed in an accident, and Court was left to handle the family business. An uncle had come to his aid to manage the accounts while Court did the work. Several years later when Court's uncle accused him of stealing funds from the business and had Court arrested, he had given him the choice of going to prison in England or going to America as an indentured servant. Court had chosen America, hoping never to lay eyes on his uncle again.

The little barrel for Kendra had been the first time Court had applied himself to his old trade since his arrival in America. Feeling the wood take shape under his fingers had been like the old days. In the evenings, after dark, Court had worked on it by candlelight. With each loving stroke he'd thought of Kendra using it to store her hairpins.

"Kendra, listen to me. We must remain strong. Let God move on our behalf with your father. If you let God's peace guard your heart, it'll help the time go easier."

"All right." Reluctantly Kendra stepped back, clutching the barrel. She pulled Turnip's reins loose and mounted. Looking down at Court's loving face, she smiled once, then turned the horse and rode back through the trees.

Kendra had to bite back the tears that burned in her throat. *I will not cry*, she told herself. Aloud, she began to pray, "Father God, I want to marry Court Yardley, but I'm not a very patient person. I've waited for two years and now that we're down to the last few months, I'm growing impatient. Please help me to walk in peace. Show us if there is anything we need to do. Amen."

Humming softly to herself, Kendra tried to enjoy the rest of her ride. She took the time to look around her. A squirrel scurried up a nearby tree as she rode past. Birds squawked at each other high in the treetops. Feeling lighthearted again, she urged Turnip into a trot when she reached the edge of the trees.

A few minutes later, she left Turnip in the barn and strolled up to the house. Brooke, Taylor's sturdy four-year-old daughter, and Daniel, Cammie's two year old, were playing near the large house as Cammie watched over them. Lifting a hand to wave at them, Kendra smiled as they shouted to her in greeting.

As she climbed the wide staircase to her bedroom, Kendra was still amazed at how beautiful it looked compared to the loft she and Laurel had had to share in the cabin. With a room of her own now, Kendra found it difficult to sleep at night without Laurel next to her. Having privacy was nice but lonely. She had been delighted and a little surprised to find that Laurel was missing her presence as well. They had laughed over their predicament. There had been many happy times in those cabins, but the spacious new house was much more pleasant.

Pulling off her gloves, Kendra walked across to the dressing table and lovingly set down the barrel from Court. Her fingers gently caressed it before she turned toward the wardrobe to change out of her riding habit. It was while she searched through her clothes that Laurel came in.

"Oh, Kendra," sighed Laurel. "I'm so happy." Gliding across the room, Laurel held the letter in her hand toward Kendra.

"What's this?" Kendra asked, glancing briefly at the paper.

"It's a letter from Clair Portland. She and Jason are coming here to visit." Leaning against the wall, Laurel smiled, the letter clutched to her chest. "I'm going to marry Jason Portland. He's coming to ask for my hand in marriage, I just know it."

"Jason Portland!" Kendra stared at her sister. "You haven't seen Jason Portland in more than two years. Why would you want to marry an English snob when there are good young men around here?"

"The only young men around here worth pursuing are the Grand twins," Laurel sniffed sarcastically.

"Saul and Simon Grand are fine young men. Either one of them would make you a good husband," Kendra replied.

The Grand family was one of their closest neighbors. They had a splendid house after which the Marstons had fashioned their own home. Saul and Simon were their only two sons. Blessed with good looks and genial personalities, the twins had long been chased by every marriageable young lady in the county.

Laurel had spent time with the young men at several social events, but with each letter she received from Clair Portland, she stiffened her resolve. One day Jason Portland would be her husband. And now she saw that the wait had been worth it. He was on his way to South Carolina at this very moment.

"Jason is the only man for me, Kendra. I don't want anyone else. There's no one on this earth who causes my heart to beat the way Jason does."

Twirling around the room, Laurel dreamily began to conjure up Jason's image. It was difficult since she'd not seen him in the past two years. He'd had golden blonde hair and the palest blue eyes. And each time he'd kissed the back of Laurel's hand, his mustache had tickled. Stroking her hand against her cheek, Laurel could almost feel the sensation now.

"What will Father say when he hears about the Portlands coming?" Slipping her gown over her head, Kendra noticed the faraway look in her sister's eyes. She hoped the mention of their father's possibly less-than-excited reaction would snap Laurel out of her daydream. It had no effect, though, and she continued, "He didn't like Jason when we were in England. Why should he change his mind now that we're here in America?"

Laurel couldn't understand her father's attitude toward Jason Portland. He'd only met him on a few occasions. Everyone seemed to like Jason except Yates Marston. Brow furrowed, Laurel began to wonder how her father would take the news of the Portlands' arrival.

"Father wouldn't dare turn guests away," Laurel insisted. "What would people think? Anyway, after Jason gets here, we'll convince Father to allow us to marry. There's no other man I wish to spend my life with."

Kendra turned for Laurel to hook up the gown, which was one of her favorites, then studied her reflection in the mirror. The short puffed sleeves of the dress left Kendra's arms bare, which was a relief after the heavy riding habit. The high waist fit snugly under her breast, while the skirt fell softly to the floor. The scooped collar, decorated with a lacy ruffle, revealed a glimpse of the curves that had developed over the last two years. She pulled on her elbow-length gloves. She broke into her sister's reverie to ask, "When are you going to tell Father?"

"I'll tell Father tonight at dinner." Laurel stubbornly stuck her chin out. "He must allow them to come!" With that, she hurried from the room.

With a sigh, Kendra followed.

Yates Marston believed in keeping things as civilized as possible. Sitting at the head of the table with his wife, Maida, on his right, Yates studied the rest of his family. His brother, Ward, and his wife, Taylor, were seated at the opposite end with little Brooke. Young Reid Marston sat to Maida's right. Kendra and Laurel sat across from Reid.

As soon as the food had been prayed over and served, Laurel jumped in with her news. "Father, I received another letter from Clair Portland today."

Yates acknowledged Laurel's words with a brief nod as he cut a large chunk of roast. Laurel pressed on. "She sends her regards to the family."

"That's nice," Yates murmured.

"There was also another item in her letter that was of interest," Laurel said, hoping to capture her father's attention. She closed her eyes, took a deep breath, and stated without further preamble, "She and her brother, Jason, are coming to America in August to visit us."

His fork halfway to his mouth, Yates turned his head to look at his daughter. "What do you mean they're coming for a visit?"

Smiling sweetly, Laurel continued, "Clair and Jason are coming to Catawba for a visit. You know, we've been writing back and forth for the past couple of years. Now they're coming to see us."

"Is this the same Jason Portland whom you desired to marry before we left England?" Yates was watching his daughter closely.

Laurel nodded.

"Have you been encouraging this young man through your letters, Laurel Marston?"

"What?" Laurel's blue eyes widened. "Father! I would never be so forward. I've been writing to his sister. I've not received a single letter from Jason. Clair is coming for a visit, and Jason is accompanying her."

Satisfied that Laurel hadn't tarnished her reputation, Yates nodded. "Fine. They'll be welcome in our home when they arrive."

"Oh, thank you, Father." Jumping from her seat, Laurel wrapped her arms around Yates's neck, hugging him tightly. She couldn't wait until next month.

Yates pulled Laurel's arms from around his neck. "I expect that you will act properly when the Portlands arrive. I wouldn't want them to think that you're any less of a lady since coming to America," he said sternly.

"I promise I'll be on my best behavior."

"Fine." Yates resumed eating his meal.

Maida had watched the exchange between her husband and stepdaughter without comment. Now she took a deep breath and cleared her throat. She had been waiting all day to present her own news to the family. Twining her fingers together in her lap, she looked around the table.

"Excuse me, everyone," she began with a squeak. Swallowing hard, she tried again. "I have some news of my own."

"What is it, Maida?" asked Reid.

Maida lifted her chin, praying silently for courage. "We will be having a new addition to our family. I am going to have a baby in January." Yates's fork once again halted in mid-air.

"A baby," squealed Kendra. "Oh, Maida, that's wonderful." Dashing around the table she threw her arms around her stepmother.

The rest of the family followed. Hugs and congratulations were enthusiastically passed around. It was a dinner of celebration. No one but Maida noticed that Yates didn't join in the festivities.

The party had been planned for months. The front parlor was being transformed into a quaint ballroom. Servants were scurrying around preparing the food and cleaning the house. It had been two weeks since Laurel had received her letter from Clair and Maida had made her announcement that the baby was coming.

Watching Laurel meticulously prepare for the party—taking a bath, washing and curling her hair, and making sure her dress was pressed properly—was enough to drive anyone from the house, and Kendra had decided to escape for a quick ride. She was glad to get away from the bustle for awhile.

Climbing into her saddle, Kendra nudged Turnip forward, knowing that there was little time. The party was only a few hours away and she'd have to begin preparing soon. But the shadowing trees beckoned to her and within moments, she was relaxing in the peace and quiet of the forest.

The faint sound of gunfire echoing through the forest jarred her from her daydream. Chattering in anger, birds flew in agitation from their resting places high in the trees.

Kendra tightened her hold on Turnip's reins. Someone must be hunting.

"Hush, Turnip," she soothed, leaning down to pat the horse's neck. "It's all right, girl."

She looked up. Great branches blocked out most of the radiant sun. The smell of pine trees and damp soil filled her nostrils. She swatted away the mosquitoes that buzzed around her head and slid from Turnip's back, the reins loosely clasped in her hands.

At that moment, a deer bounded across the path in front of her. Kendra stood frozen, astounded by the animal's beauty. The gun cracked again, much closer. Suddenly a small black girl, perspiration running down her face, dark eyes wild with fright, burst through the trees onto the path. She ran straight into Kendra, and both girls tumbled into the dirt.

From the woods came the sounds of shouting and cursing. The girl jumped up, looking frantically around for a way to escape. Kendra knew instantly the girl must be a runaway. Springing into action, she hauled the girl over to a thicket and pushed her into the middle of it.

"Don't make a sound, no matter what," Kendra whispered frantically. Seeing the girl scurry under the bushes to hide, Kendra returned to Turnip's side. She said a quick prayer for strength, and without warning, let out an ear-splitting scream and fell to the ground. She listened intently, hearing a man's shouted directions. It sounded like a herd of wild horses were coming through the trees. Closing her eyes so the men wouldn't see her fear, she groaned.

"Here," shouted the first man who came onto the path. Kneeling next to Kendra, he grabbed her roughly by the arms. "Where is she? Where's that slave girl? Did you see her?" The man was practically screaming into Kendra's face.

"I . . . I, uh, don't know where she went," she stammered. "She knocked me over." Putting a hand to her head, she moaned. "I think she went that way." As she pointed in the opposite direction from Catawba, she prayed they would believe her.

The man quickly released Kendra's arm and stood, ignoring her as she fell back against the hard ground. Two others entered the path and they engaged in a muttered discussion. No one offered Kendra a helping hand or asked if she was hurt.

Struggling to her feet, she peered at the men to see if any of them looked familiar. They were obviously very angry. She took a wary step backward, sure she did not recognize any of them.

"Are you sure she went that way, young lady?" the first man asked. When Kendra nodded, he started in the direction she had pointed, shouting orders. "Joe, you go that way. Sam, you head that way." He stabbed his finger in different directions. "If we fan out we'll trap her in the middle." Not even glancing back at Kendra, they ran into the forest.

Kendra held her breath, waiting. As the sounds of their voices faded, she knew the girl was safe—for the moment. She ran to the bush where the girl was still buried and pulled her out. "It's safe now. You can come out." The girl stood there shivering, cuts and bruises all over her face and hands. Her feet were bare, and the dress she wore, if you could call it that, was so big she needed a string at the waist to keep it in place.

"Come on." Kendra leaped into her saddle and pulled the child up behind her. She turned Turnip toward Catawba and sent her forward as fast as she dared, hoping the men were far enough away that they wouldn't hear. They were soon within sight of the plantation. Halting just before the edge of the trees, Kendra pointed.

"See that shed over there? Find a spot there and hide. Stay there until I come back for you."

Wordlessly, the girl jumped down and ran for the shed. Kendra went to the house and Taylor's room.

"Aunt Taylor?" she asked breathlessly.

Taylor looked up from the book she was reading to Brooke. Seeing Kendra's state of dishevelment, she handed Brooke to Cammie. "Cammie, will you put Brooke down for her nap, please."

"Yes, Miss Taylor. Come along, Miss Brooke, it's time for you to dream sweet dreams."

Once the door was closed, Kendra ran into Taylor's outstretched arms with a sob. Her words tumbled out over each other as, shivering with reaction, she tried to tell Taylor exactly what had happened. She suddenly realized what could have happened if she'd been caught. Taylor rubbed her back to comfort her as she gave in to the tension of the previous few moments.

"It's all right, Kendra. It's all right. God protected you. You're safe now."

Kendra wiped her tears. "I know you've helped slaves in the past, Aunt Taylor," she whispered. "I didn't know what to do with her. She's in the hay shed. What are we going to do?"

Taylor tried to think quickly. "We'll have to hide her for a few days until they stop looking for her around here. She'll be safe in the hay shed until this evening. After dark we'll move her to the hiding space." Taylor leaned closer. "Kendra, it's going to be all right. I've been doing this for more than two years. I'll see that everything is taken care of." She hesitated. "Would you like me to pray with you before you go?" At Kendra's fervent nod, Taylor bowed her head. "Father in heaven, we come to you and ask you to give us peace about this situation. You gave Kendra the courage to help this girl, and now we ask that you help her to safety. Show us where the danger is. In Jesus' name, amen."

Sniffing back tears, Kendra hugged Taylor. "Thank you, Aunt Taylor."

"You're welcome. Now, get off with you. It's going to take you a long time to get your hair straightened out before the party. Would you let Cammie know I need to speak with her, please?" Closing the door behind Kendra, Taylor sat down at her writing desk and began to make plans. She would need Court's help, but Taylor wouldn't tell Kendra that. Kendra had accidentally found out that Taylor had helped runaways, but so far she didn't know about Court. He had asked Taylor not to tell her.

Taylor remembered the first runaway she and Court had helped—Sippy. Helping her had given Taylor great satisfaction, but she never forgot the potential consequences of being caught. In the past couple of years she and Court had carefully helped a handful of mistreated slaves to go north.

Hearing the door open, Taylor turned to face Cammie. Cammie's slim form made her look much younger than her eighteen years. Most people were shocked when they discovered that she had a two-year-old son. Her long black hair was twisted into a tight knot at the back of her head. Dark skin and eyes shone brightly with a love of life. She no longer had a continual look of fear. She knew she was safe at Catawba.

Together, Cammie, Taylor, and Brooke had escaped from England and Taylor's brother-in-law, who was planning to force her to marry him. Discovering that he had intentionally killed her husband had increased Taylor's terror. Cammie had been a witness to the murder, putting her in jeopardy.

Finding a ship bound for South Carolina had been easy, but when they docked, Taylor found herself indentured to the Marston family. It had been a horrible experience, but now she was thankful. If she hadn't been indentured, she would never have met Ward Marston and become his wife.

"You wanted to see me, Missy Taylor?" Cammie asked.

"Yes, Cammie. I need you to deliver this to Court without being seen. Can you do that?"

Cammie snorted. "I been doin' for you goin' on two years. You think I goin' daft for some reason? I can do it."

Taylor laughed. "I apologize, Cammie. I know I should not underestimate you."

"Good. Now who you got to help?"

"Kendra found a runaway girl. She's hiding in the hay barn. I need Court to see that she's hidden in the special room and fed." Taylor looked sternly at Cammie. "You are not to mention a word to him about Kendra helping. Do you understand?"

Lifting her chin haughtily, Cammie looked down her nose. "Yes, Miss Taylor," she said dropping a low curtsy.

"Cammie, you are incorrigible. Now, go before it's too late. I don't want you outside after dark with the party going on tonight. You'll have to keep an eye on Brooke for me."

"Yes, ma'am."

After Cammie left, Taylor paced around the spacious room. How long could they keep this girl hidden? It didn't help matters to know that guests would be wandering around outside tonight. Court knew how to slip in and out of the shadows, but there was always a risk of being caught. And helping runaways meant instant retribution.

Laurel smiled with satisfaction at her reflection. Her blonde hair was piled high, stray curls hanging down to frame her face. The dress she wore was new, made especially for this evening. It was yellow satin with puffed sleeves and a scooped neckline. Just below her breasts was a deep yellow sash that wrapped around and tied in the back. Her slippers matched the color of her dress perfectly.

Pinching her cheeks to give them color, Laurel reached for her gloves. Fashion dictated the use of elbow-length gloves, for which she was glad. They helped hide the rough calluses on her hands. As she started to put them on, though, she shrieked.

There was a hole in the end of her left glove. She had been so careful about every detail of her outfit and now she had found a hole in her glove. Stripping it from her arm, she flung it onto a chair. Gloves might be fashionable, but they were also a nuisance. Laurel only had one pair that would be suitable for the gown she was wearing. Now what was she going to do? She scowled into the mirror for a moment, then brightened.

"Kendra has a pair exactly like these," she muttered to herself. Darting across the hall to Kendra's room, she searched through her sister's meager store of accessories and with a smile of triumph, pulled out the gloves. They were perfect, not a single hole. *Which is an absolute miracle*, Laurel thought as she put them on.

Suddenly the bedroom door opened. Turning, Laurel frowned at Kendra's disheveled appearance.

"Kendra, what have you been up to?" she exclaimed.

Starting guiltily, Kendra didn't quite meet Laurel's eyes. She pushed at her hair. She had had a nice, neat braid earlier; now most of the braid had fallen out.

Scowling, she snapped, "What are you doing in my room?"

Laurel frowned. "I came to borrow your gloves. One of mine had a hole." She lifted her hands to show Kendra the pair she was wearing.

"Oh," Kendra said, embarrassed at her outburst.

"Do you realize what time it is, Kendra? You look like you've been rolling on the ground. It's going to take you an hour just to brush through your hair." Laurel pushed her sister toward the mirror, looking over Kendra's shoulder at their reflection. "If you wish people to respect you, Kendra, you're going to have to start acting like a true lady."

"I, um, didn't realize I looked so bad," Kendra mumbled. Quickly undoing the remains of the braid, she sat at the dressing table and began brushing out her hair. Among the tangles were several dried leaves.

"Have you been disobeying Father's orders?"

Kendra's eyes snapped up instantly, catching Laurel's questioning blue gaze. "What?" Had Laurel guessed that she had helped a runaway?

"You've been trying to break one of Uncle Ward's new horses, haven't you? Even after Father forbade you to do it."

Kendra relaxed in relief. Laurel had no idea what she had done today. She allowed a small smile to lift the corners of her mouth.

"What are you smiling about, Kendra?" Laurel was watching her closely.

The smile instantly disappeared. Kendra shrugged and said the first thing she thought of. "I'm looking forward to our dinner party tonight. Aren't you?" As Laurel's eyes lighted up, Kendra knew that she had sufficiently distracted her.

Spinning around the room, her dress twisting around her legs, Laurel laughed. "Oh, Kendra, I can hardly wait. Our first formal dinner party. With the house finished we'll be able to have parties more often now. Isn't it exciting?" Humming, Laurel danced around the room as if she were in the middle of an elegant ballroom.

The mantel clock over the fireplace chimed seven. Pausing mid-dance, Laurel watched the clock until it finished. "You had better hurry, Kendra. You know Father wants us to be downstairs when our guests arrive. You have one hour to get yourself fixed up." She glanced toward the large mirror again, examining her appearance one more time. "Do you suppose all the men will want to dance with me, Kendra? I do want my dance card to be full." A dreamy smile on her face, eyes alight with excitement, Laurel glided out the door without waiting for an answer.

Kendra released the breath that she had been holding. She went to the window, her eyes searching the semi-darkness until she was able to make out the shed where the little girl was hiding. "Don't be afraid," Kendra whispered, "God is with us, and he'll get you to safety."

Closing her eyes against the darkness that spread across Catawba, Kendra thought over the events of the past hour. A small shiver ran up her back. Would those men try to track her down when they did not find the girl? Would they search through Catawba to see if the girl was hiding here?

What would Father do if he found out she had helped a runaway slave?

Her eyes flew open. What would *Court* say? Would he be angry if he knew that she was helping slaves escape from their masters? Would he hate her? Kendra slumped against the window. Would she ever be able to tell him what she had done today?

The barking of the dogs yanked Kendra sharply from her thoughts. She noticed a lantern light bobbing down the long road to Catawba. Glancing over her shoulder at the mantel clock, she yelped. There was time to worry about Court later; right now Father would be furious if she weren't downstairs on time.

Joshua Douglas tugged at the stiff collar under his chin. "Matthew, is all this clothing necessary?" he grumbled at the small black man who stood in the shadows of the room watching him. *Why do people feel the need to dress up in such uncomfortable clothing to go to dinner?* he grimaced to himself.

Matthew smiled at Joshua's antics. If he were facing death, Joshua Douglas wouldn't even flinch, but give him proper evening attire, and he was reduced to a complaining boy.

"Don't just stand there laughing at me like an old fool. Get over here and loosen this thing up." Stabbing restless fingers through jet black hair, Joshua absentmindedly messed up the slick style that Matthew had worked so hard to create. Deep, sea-blue eyes closed in irritation as Matthew worked on the knot under his chin. He felt as if he were being strung up for a hanging.

Barely reaching to the middle of Joshua's chest, Matthew had to look up to work on the tie. "Would you stan' still, boy," his deep voice rumbled.

"How much longer you gonna be, old man?"

"If you would hush your mouth long enough for me to do this, I'd not take so long. There, that's it." Matthew stepped back to survey his work. He was impressed.

Joshua Douglas was a handsome man and looked striking in his evening finery. His dark clawhammer tailcoat covered a buff-colored waistcoat. Underneath was a second waistcoat of silk. Tucked smoothly underneath was the hated cravat. Tan breeches hugged muscular thighs above shiny black boots.

"You'll pass, boy."

Joshua smiled at the gruffness of Matthew's words. Tugging at the coat, he looked in the mirror to see the outcome of the older man's work, staring for a moment at his reflection. Then, shaking his head, he walked toward the door.

"Don't forget you suppose to be a gentleman," snapped Matthew behind him. "And treat the ladies with respect."

Matthew's words wiped the smile from Joshua's face. Ladies. The very word made him sick. He couldn't stand proper ladies. Maybe they looked beautiful with their lavish gowns and jewels, but underneath they were dull as dirt. "Don't start," he growled.

"No, boy, don't you go gettin' in a foul mood before the party," Matthew reprimanded. "I knows how you feel, but don't go makin' things up in your head before you see a nice woman."

Joshua made no comment as he slammed the door behind him and Matthew chuckled softly as he walked around picking up the mess Joshua had left behind. *That boy sure hates proper ladies,* he shook his head, *but it's 'bout time for him to get over the past.*

Actually, if it hadn't been for a proper lady, he and Joshua might never have met. After five years of being with Joshua, Matthew still didn't know the full story—it was a subject that Matthew knew he was not permitted to bring up—but whatever had happened, Joshua had been deeply hurt. And it had brought them together.

Joshua had been angry and heartbroken and looking for an outlet for his rage that night. He had run into a rough-looking group of trappers; it hadn't taken much to get them riled. Matthew had stood across the street watching the incident unravel. He had been surprised at the young man's gumption. Joshua had held his own longer than expected, but, noticing the trappers weren't letting up after he fell, Matthew had known he had to help. Even though a black man fighting alongside a white man was inconceivable, he'd joined the melee.

After only a few well-directed swings, Matthew had been able to drag Joshua's bruised and unconscious body away. He'd carried him into the woods. He'd had to hide more for his own sake than for Joshua's. Because even though Matthew was a free man, if he were caught fighting white men, he would be in serious trouble. Struggling to a hiding place, he'd tended Joshua's wounds, which were severe. They had hidden for almost a month before Joshua was ready to leave.

They had never discussed their future plans, but when Joshua left, Matthew was with him.

Marissa and Jacob Ferguson stood in the doorway of Catawba waiting to be welcomed. The father and daughter were a striking pair. Jacob was a large, heavyset man with reddish brown hair and deep brown eyes. Marissa was a female version of her father, the only difference being her much more feminine figure.

Marissa's eyes glittered as she caught sight of Taylor and Ward Marston. It was a pity that Ward had married his bond servant. Now that he had made Catawba a success, Marissa would have gladly received his attentions. But who was to say that something couldn't be done about that, she thought to herself with a smirk. She had certainly been enjoying trying.

Arms linked, the Fergusons stepped forward to greet Yates and Maida, who stood first in line. Soft music was drifting out to the entryway where candles glimmered, giving it a warm, welcoming aura. The hum of conversation added to the gaiety of the evening. Everyone was bright and happy in their party finery.

"Yates, this place has definitely shaped up since you've been here," Jacob Ferguson's voice boomed out. His broad smile showed off his gold tooth. After pumping Yates's hand, Jacob turned and bowed over Maida's hand, grazing her knuckles with his lips.

"Good evening, Mr. Ferguson." Maida demurely accepted the gentlemanly attention. "Marissa."

"Good evening, Maida. You look lovely this evening," commented Marissa, prodding her father forward until she stood in front of Ward. "Good evening, Ward."

"Good evening, Marissa. I'm glad you and your father were able to make it," said Ward, bending over her extended hand.

"I wouldn't have missed it for anything." Marissa smoothed back a wisp of her auburn hair. She smiled sweetly at Ward, dimples appearing in both cheeks. "Your house is beautiful," she exclaimed, placing her hand on Ward's arm.

"I'm glad you like it," he remarked absently.

"Good evening, Marissa."

Tearing her eyes away from Ward, Marissa turned toward Taylor. "Good evening, Taylor." Scanning the woman from head to toe, Marissa wondered again how Ward could have married her. The gown she wore was just a simple high-waisted, short-sleeved satin. There were no bows, lace, or ruffles anywhere. It looked as though it belonged to a lower-class woman, which was exactly what Taylor was.

Marissa's own gown was an expensive creation from Paris. She refused to wear anything but the best. Made of peach silk, it highlighted her reddish brown hair. The low-cut neckline was extremely daring, leaving little to the imagination, and the small ruffle that followed the neckline only enhanced the creamy skin of her breasts. Her shawl helped conceal the low scoop from her father. He would have made her change it immediately.

Raising her chin a fraction of an inch, Marissa passed by Taylor without another glance.

"Isn't this wonderful, Marissa. Our very first dinner party," Laurel enthused, hugging Marissa.

"Yes, dear, it's marvelous." Marissa accepted the hug graciously.

Kendra was next. Marissa could see the fire in her eyes. Smiling falsely, she didn't bother hugging the younger girl. "Hello, Kendra. You look so . . . ," Marissa studied her from head to toe, "sweet."

"Marissa," Kendra greeted her through gritted teeth. "Don't you look . . . daring." She stiffened at the sound of Marissa's throaty laughter.

"I'm glad you noticed, Kendra. Because if you did, then so will all the young men."

"Out to snag a husband, are you?" Kendra prodded.

"Why would I want a husband? That would only keep the men from flocking to me."

Kendra held back her retort. Marissa had a way of riling her. Her attitude toward people was appalling. Kendra had tried to get Laurel to see what Marissa was really like, but it had never worked.

A gasp from Laurel caused both Marissa and Kendra to turn. Laurel's gaze was riveted on the front door and the man who stood there.

How interesting, Marissa thought, her gaze flickering from Laurel's face to the man who was now giving his cloak and gloves to a servant. *Such a handsome man . . . and without a female companion.* She noted that Laurel was still devouring the stranger with her eyes. *Poor Laurel. She doesn't even realize that this one is out of her league. But not out of mine.* Laurel didn't notice the thoughtful smile that crossed her friend's face.

Laurel grew very still as she caught sight of the man who stood in the entryway. He was taller than Ward, with shoulders so broad that Laurel grew weak-kneed at the sight of them. His black hair was slightly ruffled, as if he had run his fingers through it. His sweeping gaze moved down the row of the Marston family.

Laurel couldn't tear her eyes away. She vaguely heard Marissa ask Kendra if she knew who the man was. The music fading into the background, Laurel only had eyes for the tall, dark-haired stranger.

"Laurel. Laurel!" Kendra frowned at her sister. What was the matter with her? Didn't she realize she was making a spectacle of herself? Wrapping her fingers around Laurel's arm, Kendra squeezed until she saw Laurel wince.

"What's the matter with you?" Kendra hissed. When Laurel only stared at her blankly, Kendra shook her arm sharply. Knowing only one thing that would jar her sister out of her trancelike state, she whispered, "You're not acting like a proper lady."

The words were like a cold bucket of water. Lifting her chin, Laurel tore her eyes from the stranger.

Marissa's eyes gleamed at Laurel's reaction to the man before them. *How interesting*, she thought, her mouth slanting into a wicked smile. *Little Laurel really seems taken with him. What would she do if I were to attract his attention? Would she be angry or would she just let me have him?* Marissa decided to find out.

Ward stepped forward and clasped the man's hand in a firm grip. "I'm glad you were able to make it, Joshua. Everyone, this is Joshua Douglas, who just bought a farm across the way from us." He introduced him to the family one by one, finally reaching Kendra and Laurel.

"These are my nieces, Laurel and Kendra. Ladies, I would like you to meet our new neighbor, Joshua Douglas."

Laurel watched Joshua's dark head lean over her extended hand. His lips left a strange yearning inside her. Controlling a sudden urge to touch his hair, she stiffened. "Good evening, Mr. Douglas," she said primly.

Stepping forward, Kendra dropped a short curtsy. "How do you do, Mr. Douglas?" She looked him right in the eyes and was surprised to see laughter in their blue depths. "Where is your land, Mr. Douglas?" she questioned boldly.

"He purchased Bromley's old place," Ward answered before Joshua was able to speak.

An inarticulate sound escaped Laurel's throat as her hand flew up to her mouth. She could not control the shiver that shook her slender frame.

It had taken her more than a year to quench the memories of the horrible day when Alden Bromley had kidnapped Maida from Catawba. They had gone to fetch her back and Bromley had chased them, crazed with anger. He had actually shot his long rifle at Kendra, but it had misfired. In that split second, Laurel had aimed her own rifle and shot him, killing him instantly. She still had occasional nightmares about that day.

Joshua frowned. "Is something wrong?" he questioned. *What has caused the proper little lady to turn so pale?* he wondered.

"It's nothing, Douglas," assured Ward, trying to cover the awkward silence. "The man was not well liked by the women here at Catawba."

Nodding as if he understood, Joshua turned toward Marissa. "And who is this lovely creature?" he asked. Stepping forward to take her hand, he pressed his lips briefly to her knuckles. Marissa's cheeks flushed prettily as she smiled, deepening her dimples, and Ward quickly introduced Joshua to her. "I seem to have lost my escort, Mr. Douglas," she cooed. "Would you mind accompanying me inside?"

"I would enjoy nothing more, Miss Ferguson." Joshua pulled her slender fingers through his arm. He was well aware that this coy young woman was trying to work her feminine wiles on him, and he was perfectly willing to play along. At least it would lessen the tedium of the evening.

As they stepped away from the group, Joshua heard Kendra whisper, "Don't let the mention of Alden Bromley ruin this perfect evening, Laurel." His curiosity was piqued. Miss Laurel Marston was not of consequence to him, but her reaction to the mention of Bromley was intriguing. He'd have Matthew check into it for him.

Alden Bromley. The name kept ringing through Laurel's mind as she absently watched Marissa walk away with Joshua Douglas. Vaguely she heard Kendra tell her not to let it ruin the evening, but nothing could stop the images that flashed through her mind so vividly. Images of Bromley's enraged face as he lifted his rifle . . . of Taylor and Kendra's fearstruck faces . . . and of the surprise on Alden's face as she shot him. . . .

Laurel shivered and forcibly dragged her thoughts from the dark hole into which they were descending and back to the party. As the family finished greeting their guests, she was almost her usual calm self. Nothing was going to ruin her evening. There were plenty of young men to dance with and she was going to enjoy every moment of it.

She looked around. Groups of people stood scattered about the room. The strains of a waltz covered their murmuring voices. Large French doors stood open to the veranda, allowing a small breeze to cool the crowded room, and chairs and sofas lined the walls, comfortable seating for those who wished. A large buffet table stretched across one long wall. Hundreds of candles illuminated the whole affair.

Strolling from group to group, Laurel found her gaze drawn toward Joshua Douglas. Marissa's hand was snuggled into the crook of his arm. Their heads were close together and Laurel heard the delicate sound of Marissa's laughter as Joshua spoke. An ache, deep inside, made Laurel turn away from the couple.

Before she could analyze her feelings, though, Saul Grand came to claim Laurel for the next dance. The fast pace of the music and intricate steps kept her thoughts from drifting and by the time the music stopped and she was claimed by her next partner, she had determined that no one, least of all the enigmatic Mr. Douglas, was going to keep her from enjoying the festive occasion. She gave herself up to the company of the attractive young men who had signed her dance card.

It wasn't until she had twirled from one partner to another for several hours that Laurel finally claimed exhaustion and, accepting a glass of punch, quietly slipped through the door for a moment alone. Only a few people wandered around the lawn, taking advantage of the beautiful evening. Not wanting to be disturbed, she sat in a chair hidden behind a large pillar and took a sip of her punch.

It wasn't cool outside, but without the sun beating down it was refreshing. Muffled sounds from the party drifted through the French doors. So intent was she on the lovely night and atmosphere, Laurel didn't notice the footsteps bringing intruders closer to her hiding place until they were almost on top of her. Holding her breath, she hoped they would pass by. She wasn't ready to return to the party quite yet. When the steps stopped just on the other side of the pillar, she heaved a sigh of relief.

"So tell me, Joshua, what brought you to this area?" she heard Marissa Ferguson's voice.

Laurel wanted to sink through the ground. Of all the people at the party, why had Marissa and Joshua been the ones to intrude upon her sanctuary? There was nothing she could do. She couldn't make her presence known without embarrassment, but neither did Laurel care to eavesdrop on the private conversation.

On the other side of the pillar, Joshua was smiling down at his companion. "I was ready to settle down to a home of my own, Miss Ferguson."

Pouting prettily, Marissa lay her hand on Joshua's arm. "I told you to call me Marissa. All my friends do—and I consider you one of my friends." She smiled up at him suggestively.

"Very well, Marissa."

"Now isn't that much better?" Marissa stepped closer, sliding her hands up the front of Joshua's snug jacket. Her head tilted back and slightly to the side. She knew this gave her handsome partner a good view of her slender neck and the revealing scoop of her neckline. "Does your settling down mean that you're looking for a wife?"

Joshua regarded Marissa closely. "Are you volunteering yourself for the position?" he asked silkily, with the tiniest trace of sarcasm.

Laurel almost gasped aloud at their bold words. How could Marissa be so forward with a complete stranger? No proper lady would act as she was acting. Putting a hand over her mouth to stifle her reaction, she continued listening.

Batting her eyes up at Joshua, Marissa pressed herself closer until Joshua's arms automatically wrapped around her. "That all depends on what you have to offer me," she stated boldly.

Joshua's rumbling laughter wiped the smile from her face. "Are you laughing at me, Joshua Douglas?" she protested.

"No, Marissa, I'm not laughing at you," he said, playfully tugging one of her curls. "I'm laughing at myself. There's not much I can offer you at this time, so I think we'll have to drop this conversation for a while."

"Oh, very well," she pouted. "On one condition."

"And what, pray tell, would that be?"

"A kiss."

"Excuse me?"

"Don't act so shocked, Joshua. All I want is a little kiss." Marissa slid her arms around Joshua's neck, pulling his head down. "I'm sure you won't be disappointed."

Joshua smiled at her. "My daddy always told me to give a lady anything she wants."

Behind the pillar, Laurel sat as if made of stone, a deep flush heating her face. Joshua Douglas might be a handsome man, but he was no gentleman. And to think she'd been attracted to him! With each moment of silence, her frown grew deeper. Just how long was this kiss going to last? The quiet was finally broken with a deep sigh.

"That was wonderful," Marissa murmured.

Without a reply, Joshua dropped his arms and stepped back. "I believe we should go in now, Miss Ferguson. I wouldn't want to be responsible for tarnishing your reputation." A frown marred his dark face. Usually he was amused by the women that vied for his attentions. A brief kiss here and there never hurt anyone. But this time, he hadn't enjoyed it as he usually did.

Marissa giggled. "Don't worry about my reputation, Mr. Douglas," she stated formally. "I take good care of it."

"I'm sure you do." Joshua gave a small bow. "Why don't you precede me in and I shall follow shortly? That way there will be no questions."

"Very well," Marissa concurred. "I shall wait for you inside."

Hearing Marissa's retreating steps, Laurel quietly peeked around the pillar. She hoped with all her heart that Mr. Douglas had walked to another area so she could return to the party.

"You can come out now, Miss Marston."

With a horrified gasp, Laurel stood. Her now-empty punch glass slipped from her grasp to shatter on the floor. She was mortified. Without thought to her gown, she dropped to her knees and began picking up the pieces.

"Be careful," Joshua warned sharply, dropping down beside her. "You could cut yourself."

"This is terrible. Just terrible. What am I going to do?"

Laurel completely forgot about Joshua Douglas in her distress over the broken glass. It was from a set that had been passed down from mother to daughter for three generations. Laurel remembered the day she had been allowed to hold one of the cups for the first time. The set was the only thing she had that had belonged to her mother. Unshed tears blurred her vision, making it difficult to see the small shards of glass and with a gasp of pain, she held up a bleeding finger.

"Now look what you've done," Joshua said harshly. Snatching Laurel's hand, he stripped the glove from her arm and held the bleeding finger toward the light spilling from the door. Carefully he felt for the small sliver of glass. Laurel hissed between her teeth as his calloused finger found the hidden intruder and pulled it out. He lifted his head.

Laurel's eyes widened as she found herself staring into a pair of deep, blue eyes. Her breath caught as Joshua stared down at her expressionlessly. Then, without a word, he brought Laurel's injured finger to his lips and kissed it tenderly.

Laurel sat spellbound, staring at Joshua's lips on her hand. A tingling sensation started at the tip of her finger and slowly spread up her arm. She had never dreamed that the mere touch of a man could wreak such havoc on her senses. Time seemed to stand still as they knelt together in the dark.

It was the memory of those same lips kissing Marissa Ferguson only moments earlier that brought Laurel back to her senses. Jerking her hand free, she reached for her abandoned glove and tugged it back on, hoping there were no bloodstains.

"Thank you for your help, sir," she said stiffly.

"My pleasure, Miss Marston." Joshua's brow lifted at her rigid response. He hadn't expected such coolness. With an almost imperceptible shrug, he rose to assist her. Laurel knew there was no way she could refuse his help without seeming rude. She reached for the pile of glass resting on her gown.

"No," Joshua barked. Kneeling again, he swept the pieces onto the floor. "You don't want to hurt yourself again, do you?"

"Uh . . . no." Laurel could only blink at him. Taking his outstretched hand, she stood. "Thank you, Mr. Douglas," she muttered.

"You're welcome, Miss Marston." With a slight bow, Joshua turned and left.

The whole incident had taken only moments, but Laurel was stunned as she stood staring at Joshua's retreating back. What a strange man he was. She would have never guessed at the tenderness he'd shown in that fleeting instant. And the sensations that tenderness had evoked—Laurel didn't even want to dwell on that.

Jason will make me feel the same way, she reasoned. *Surely all kisses are the same. I'll enjoy Jason's just as much.*

She hoped with all her heart that it was true.

The evening was warm, yet a slight breeze wafted through the open doors. Candles glowed, lighting the entire room. Musicians were positioned in a far corner, playing softly. Elegant gowns twirled around the dance floor in time with the music.

Taylor stood beside Ward with her ears pricked. She had been hoping to get some information this evening about the runaway slave that Kendra had brought home. So far she hadn't heard a word . . . until now.

". . . the girl was worth quite a bit, I understand." Glancing to her right, Taylor noticed a small group of men. Were they discussing the runaway girl?

Leaning close to Ward, Taylor whispered. "I'll be right back." Trying not to act overly eager, she moved to mingle with a group near the men. She listened closely.

"Do they know where she's at?" asked one of the men.

"Nope."

"Probably fell into the swamp."

"I don't know. There are those people that help runaways. Maybe some of them are around here."

Taylor stiffened. Did anyone suspect her? Would she be caught? She forced herself to remain calm.

"Now who would be that crazy?"

"Who did she belong to?"

"Some big man that's just moved into the area. The men hunting her said he would make certain that anyone caught helping her would be severely punished."

"But you don't know his name?"

"Nope."

The group turned toward Joshua. Taylor followed their gaze. A small shiver shot through her. Joshua Douglas? Was the girl's owner here at Catawba? This was too frightening. Excusing herself, Taylor returned to Ward's side. She felt safer beside him. Her mind whirled with questions. Joshua Douglas had just moved into the area. Ward had told her that much. He didn't look like a cruel person, but some people were good at hiding their true personality. Caught up in her thoughts, Taylor didn't notice Ward's scrutiny until he spoke.

"Are you all right, Taylor?"

Taylor tried to look lighthearted, but failed. Clasping her hand, Ward brought it to the crook of his arm and took her toward the door. Darkness closed around them.

"What's wrong, my love?" he asked gently.

"I was just wondering how it came about that you met Joshua Douglas."

"Joshua?" Surprised, Ward frowned in thought. "I met him in town. Why?"

"Then you don't know anything about him?" Dropping her voice, Taylor glanced toward the door. No one was there.

Ward shook his head. "No. He told me where his place was, and since he's our closest neighbor, I invited him. Have you heard something?"

"No."

What could Taylor say? She had overheard a conversation that left little doubt in her mind that Joshua Douglas was a cruel man. But she wasn't certain. She didn't want to say such awful things about a man if they weren't true.

"Taylor," Ward warned, "you'd better tell me the truth." Taylor had never been very good at lying. She looked Ward right in the eye.

"I don't know anything for sure. I don't like to repeat gossip, and it's probably completely untrue."

Chuckling, Ward bent quickly and kissed Taylor on the lips. "I love you, Mrs. Marston."

Taylor would have collapsed in his strong arms if he hadn't broken away from her just as quickly. The warmth of his lips brought the smile back to her face. "I love you too, Mr. Marston."

Sliding his arm around her small waist, Ward took Taylor back to the party.

Lizy hunched in the far corner of the hay barn. The commotion of carriages entering and people talking and laughing frightened her. Perspiration ran down her brown skin. Her gasping breaths seemed so loud that she felt certain someone would find her.

Closing her dark eyes, she silently mouthed a prayer. Her childish fingers clasped her oversized rag of a dress around her shoulders. At thirteen, her body beginning to develop, she was thankful for this dress. Lately, Lizy had known that if her true age were discovered, the overseer would force his attentions on her. Her thin, wiry body had always looked younger than her years. But as she grew up, the charade had almost ended. Finding this dress had been her salvation.

The overseer didn't like Lizy or her uppity talk. She tried to keep her mouth shut, but she couldn't help herself. The last beating he gave her had almost killed her, so she had decided it was time to leave her family behind and run. She just had to wait until her body was healed enough to make the journey north.

But before she could escape, the overseer had discovered the secret that her dress had hidden for so long. Her terror that he would come for her that night had forced her to flee immediately. Without looking back, she had run into the night and the swamp, where she'd hidden under some brush until daylight. At first light, she'd begun to run again.

She had been so frightened. Those men had almost caught her. She had thought it was over when she ran into the white lady. Yet, instead of screaming at her, the pretty girl had shoved her under a bush to hide. If Lizy hadn't been so afraid that the men would find her, she would have laughed at the way the white girl had thrown herself on the ground screaming. But the men had believed the girl when she'd told them which way Lizy had run. That was all that mattered.

As Lizy sat inside the barn, deep in thought, a dark shadow moved stealthily outside it. *This is the one*, it thought. *It has to be.* Easing the door open quietly, the figure slipped in undetected. Where was she? She had to be here somewhere.

Intent on silence, the shadow stepped around several stacks of hay then paused, waiting, listening. Was that a gasp it had heard? Was the girl right there? A tentative hand reached out, feeling in the dark. Where was she?

Mere feet away, Lizy fought to keep from screaming. She hadn't heard a sound, but her instincts told her that someone else was in the barn. Tense with fear, she strained to see in the dark. Who was there? She dared not breathe. They would kill her if they found her.

After a moment's intense silence, she couldn't take it anymore. She had to get out. Jumping to her feet, she leaped from her hiding place and ran. What she couldn't see in the dark, though, was a man standing directly in her path to freedom. Instead of running toward safety, Lizy found herself caught in strong arms. Kicking and clawing, she fought to escape. They might kill her for running, but they would have some bruises to remember her by.

Muscular arms wrapped around Lizy's flailing frame, trapping her arms at her sides. Tears of frustration fell down her cheeks. In the dark silence, Lizy's sob seemed to scream through the night.

"Ssssh," hissed the shadow.

Trying to control her ragged breathing, Lizy obeyed instantly. What was he going to do with her?

"I'm here to help you," he whispered against her ear. Leaning even closer he continued. "I'm taking you to a safe place, but you have to be very quiet."

Her small body relaxed slightly.

"Are you ready?"

Nodding her head silently, Lizy felt drained. She wanted to curl up and fall asleep without fear of being caught. Would she really be safe with this man? He took Lizy by the hand, and they walked silently through the night until they came to a larger barn. Instead of opening the big front doors, though, they slipped through a side door covered by shadows.

Saddles, harnesses, ropes, bridles, and tools lined the shelves and hung from the walls. The man walked over to one of the tables and slid it to one side. He leaned over and pulled at the floor. There was a trapdoor there. Easing the well-oiled hinges back, he leaned it against another work table, climbed quickly down the ladder, and then helped Lizy down. Not a single sliver of light shone in the underground room.

"My name is Court," he whispered. "What's yours?"

"Lizy."

"Well, Lizy, this is our saferoom. There's a bed and food down here. You should get some sleep. I'll come back for you soon." Without another word, Court mounted the ladder and closed the door softly behind him.

Lizy peered into the darkness hoping to catch sight of the bed, but she couldn't see anything. Crouching down, she stretched out her hand and slowly made her way around the room until she bumped into the frame. With a sigh, she lay down and fell asleep.

Upstairs, Court returned everything in the tack room to its proper place and stepped out into the darkness with a sigh of relief. He looked up into the sky, mouthed a silent prayer for Lizy, then chuckled as he thought about the kick she'd given him when he caught her. She had felt like skin and bones, but she was strong. Court prayed that she would make it to freedom.

Joshua slowly mounted the stairs of his home. The evening's festivities had been enjoyable but taxing. Marissa Ferguson had been very entertaining. After the way she had flirted with him there was no doubt in his mind that she was not a proper young lady.

Joshua was surprised to see Matthew waiting up for him. "Why aren't you in bed, Matthew?"

The older man shrugged. "Wanted to see how the party went."

Joshua laughed. "Don't worry, old man, I acted like a perfect gentleman in front of all the proper ladies."

Matthew grumbled as he began hanging up the clothes Joshua discarded. "You just haven't met the right lady yet."

With the word *lady*, Laurel Marston's image invaded Joshua's mind. The incident with her had plagued his thoughts all evening. Finding her sitting on the other side of the pillar had been unfortunate. He was sure she'd heard everything that had transpired between himself and Marissa. He didn't like the thought of her listening in, but there was nothing he could do about that now. He certainly hadn't intended to kiss her finger. A desire to stop the pain was all he'd had in mind. Her reaction to the kiss was typical of a prim little lady, though. Yes, she was a proper lady. There was no doubt about that.

"What you thinkin' so hard about?" Matthew asked.

"A certain lady," Joshua commented sarcastically.

"Oh?" Matthew waited for Joshua to fill in the details. When he didn't continue, he looked closely at Joshua's face.

Noticing Matthew's stare, Joshua cleared his throat and changed the subject.

"There's a little something I want you to check into," he said. "The previous owner of this land, Alden Bromley, had a run-in with the Marstons. I want you to find out what happened."

"He stole one of the women," Matthew stated matter-of-factly.

"What?" Joshua asked in astonishment.

"I believe it was the black-haired one, Miss Maida."

"How do you know that?" Joshua asked suspiciously.

Matthew smiled. "I'm curious and people like to talk to me."

Sitting down in a chair near the fireplace, Joshua motioned for Matthew to sit with him. "All right, tell me everything you know."

"It seems Master Bromley was upset with the other married woman, Miss Taylor. He hired some men to kidnap her, only they got the wrong woman. Well, the Marstons looked and looked for her, but couldn't find her 'cause Bromley had her hidden.

"One of his slaves, though, liked Miss Taylor and told her where to find the woman. She and the other two girls came to fetch her home. When Bromley found her gone, he went crazy. He stopped them on the road and tried to shoot one of the girls, but his gun was empty and Miss Laurel shot him dead."

"What?" Joshua exclaimed.

"That's what I heard," Matthew stated, shrugging his shoulder.

Tipping his head back, Joshua tried to think. *How could Laurel Marston have shot a man? That's too incredible to believe.* He shook his head. *That proper little lady shooting a man?*

Taylor lay staring up at the ceiling of her room. Ward's soft snores helped soothe the turmoil in her mind. It seemed like one problem after another was weighing her down. The worst one now was Marissa Ferguson.

Tonight had actually been a relief for Taylor. Joshua Douglas had unknowingly kept Marissa away from Ward. The younger woman took every opportunity to get Ward alone, ostensibly to discuss horses. That was Ward's passion, and Marissa encouraged him to talk to her at length about it.

Men are so blind. How can Ward not see what that woman is doing? Taylor wondered. At first it had been amusing to watch Marissa practically throw herself at Ward. He never took notice, so Taylor didn't mind. But recently the situation had changed.

Several weeks ago, Taylor had gone to the barn seeking her husband. Walking in, she had been shocked at the sight of Marissa's arms around Ward's neck. Her pretty mouth had been pouting up at him. Without a sound, Taylor had turned and fled.

That was the turning point for her. After dropping a few hints to Ward, she realized that he still wasn't aware of Marissa's intentions. When Taylor confronted him directly about the scene in the barn he'd been nothing but surprised. It seemed Marissa had almost fallen over a bucket near the stable. She had reached for Ward to steady herself.

When Taylor pointed out Marissa's constant attentions toward him, Ward had responded with a laugh. He didn't believe Marissa was infatuated with him. Taylor realized she would have to keep an eye on Marissa herself. No one was going to take her husband from her.

Taylor rolled onto her side, snuggling closer to Ward. She hoped Court had gotten the runaway girl into the saferoom. Tomorrow would be soon enough to tackle that problem. Finding out the details about the girl wasn't going to be easy.

She and Court had decided that they should only help runaways who were abused by their masters. Most of the plantations in the area treated their slaves well, encouraging them to have families, so they didn't get many deserters. But now it seemed that Joshua Douglas was the cause of this girl's escape attempt. They would have to be very careful.

Taylor didn't have any peace about helping this girl. Something wasn't right, but she didn't know exactly what. She knew that slave owners and lawmen sometimes convinced slaves to expose those who helped runaways. From Kendra's description, though, this girl was too young to be involved in something like that . . . Taylor hoped. No, there had to be something else. She sighed and lifted a prayer to heaven.

Father, you alone know everything about this situation. Show me how to find out what it is. Thank you for your wisdom and guidance in everything I do. Amen.

Kendra bounded out of bed and across the room, throwing on the first gown her hand touched. She had slept past the breakfast hour, and she couldn't wait to speak with Taylor. The runaway was supposed to have been taken care of last night, but she wanted to make sure.

After learning Taylor's whereabouts, Kendra ran down the hill to the barn. It was dimly lit, and the air had a musty odor that stung her nostrils. "Aunt Taylor," called Kendra.

"Over here."

Kendra found Taylor and Brooke with a mare who had given birth a few days earlier. The small, brown colt was standing on spindly legs.

"Aunt Kendra, look at the horse," piped Brooke. Standing on the bottom rail of the stall, she leaned over the rails to get a good look. Her pink cotton dress was streaked with dirt, and the cotton tights covering her little legs drooped around her knees and ankles. A bow held her soft brown hair back, leaving a long curl to hang in the middle of her back. The older women smiled as her childish laughter gurgled through the barn.

Kendra turned back to Taylor. "Can I speak with you, Aunt Taylor?" she asked.

Taylor nodded. "Did you enjoy the party last night?" she asked.

"It was wonderful," Kendra exclaimed. "I loved the music and dancing the best."

"Was your dance card full?"

Kendra shrugged. "Not as full as Laurel's."

Taylor smiled fondly at her niece. Although she loved both her nieces dearly, she had a special place in her heart for Kendra. Her experience as an indentured servant had been made bearable with Kendra's friendship. "You'll have full dance cards one day. You won't have to worry about that."

"It doesn't matter. I'm not interested in any of the young men, but I do like to dance." Clasping her hands together, Kendra laid them in her lap. She wished she could talk to Taylor about her feelings for Court.

"Aunt Taylor," Kendra whispered, "how is our little friend?"

"She's fine, Kendra. Her name is Lizy, and she's been settled in the hidden room."

"Is she going to be all right?"

Taylor frowned. "I don't know. She has a lot of fear for one so small, but with God's help we'll get her safely up north."

"Have you spoken with her?"

"No. Someone else is taking care of her."

"Who?"

"I can't tell you that, Kendra. It is better that you don't know."

"But why?"

Taylor sighed. "It's for your own safety that I don't tell you about anyone else involved. If anything should happen, you would be able to plead ignorance along with the rest of the family. Do you understand?"

"Yes."

"I know this isn't easy, but it's necessary." When Kendra nodded, Taylor continued, "Now, I need to discuss something with you. Lizy won't tell us who she belongs to because she's afraid we'll send her back. Last evening, I overheard some gentlemen talking, and from my assessment I believe her master may be Joshua Douglas."

"What?" Kendra almost shouted.

"Calm down, Kendra, I don't know if it is true. We can't judge the man until we know for sure."

Taylor related the conversation she had overheard and the suspicions she had regarding Joshua. "You realize, Kendra, that there's nothing we can do even if he does abuse his slaves. By law they belong to him."

"They belong to him, but we'll help them get away if they want," Kendra said firmly. "If Lizy won't talk to us, how will we find out if he's the one?"

"That's the dilemma."

Kendra paced a short distance back and forth thinking. "What if we found out from Joshua Douglas himself?"

"I don't think the man will admit that he's beating his slaves. If we were men, he might boast to us, but it would not be proper conversation for ladies to hear," Taylor pointed out.

"We could spend time with him," Kendra suggested, "then bring the subject up in idle conversation."

"You mean spy on him?" Taylor asked.

"Precisely. If we can get him to talk to us openly, we may find out the truth."

"I don't know, Kendra," Taylor said shaking her head.

"Uncle Ward mentioned that Joshua Douglas wanted to learn about training horses. He offered to show Mr. Douglas around. That would give us the perfect opportunity to get to know him."

Taylor considered this. "How would it help us if Ward is showing him around?"

"Do you think you could persuade Uncle Ward to let me show him the horses?"

"I guess it's possible," Taylor said hesitantly, then rushed on. "But, Kendra, this isn't a game. If the man is as cruel as they said, you shouldn't be around him."

"We need to find out the truth."

"All right. I'll try. But I hope we're wrong about Mr. Douglas."

Maida hesitated outside Yates's office door. *I have to talk to him*, she encouraged herself. *I can't let him pretend that this baby isn't really coming. He's got to face it sooner or later, and it would be much better for it to be now.*

Her decision to tell the whole family together had been difficult. Maida and Yates had never talked about having children. And since Yates's first wife and baby had died during childbirth, Maida had known he would be anxious about her news. She had thought it would be easier for him if the family was excited when he heard. Apparently not.

Now, a total of three weeks had passed since her announcement. Still Yates refused to discuss the matter.

Squaring her shoulders, Maida firmly knocked on the door and entered. "Yates, may I speak with you?" she asked.

With a frown, Yates glanced up from the letter he was writing. He motioned to a chair in front of his desk and returned to his work. The pen scratched rapidly over the paper. Maida sat stiffly in the chair, not saying a word. She would wait until Yates gave her his full attention before speaking. She was not going to leave this room until he talked to her.

Finally laying his pen aside, Yates looked up. "What do you need, Maida?"

"Some of your time," she stated. He knew why she was here. Maida could see it in his eyes.

"Must it be now?" he asked impatiently.

"Yes."

With a sigh Yates nodded. "Very well."

Sympathy for her husband softened Maida's words. "Yates, I love you. And I want to give you children." She placed her hands over her belly. "This is a symbol of that love, and we both need to share in the joy of it."

Yates jerked to his feet. Walking to the window, he stared out over Catawba. "Why didn't you tell me first?" he murmured.

Maida's heart plummeted at the anguish in his voice. Moving to stand behind him, she leaned her head against his back. With a deep sigh she tried to explain. "I knew it would be difficult for you to handle the news. Telling everyone together, I thought, would help you adjust to the idea with less heartache."

Turning Yates to face her, Maida looked into his eyes. "Yates, I am not Ellen. Just because she died giving birth doesn't mean the same will happen to me."

"I don't want to lose you, Maida," he whispered. Pulling her roughly into his arms, he crushed her small body against him.

Maida couldn't move. The desperation in his hold relayed his misery. Tears rolled down her cheeks. It no longer mattered that Yates had treated her poorly at the beginning of their marriage. He had come to love her intensely. Maida had no doubts about that now.

"Yates," she pleaded, "you can't live with this fear forever. You've got to let it go. The Bible says that fear is not from God. Please, for the sake of this child, let God heal you."

Gentle fingers glided along Maida's jaw. Tenderness glowed in Yates's deep brown eyes. "Will you help me, Maida?" he begged.

Maida wrapped her arms around him. Silently she prayed for her husband. She had hoped this baby would help them get over the only thing that stood between them: Yates's fear of death.

"Father, help me," Yates prayed. "I don't want to be afraid any longer. Show me how to release my fear and not let it rule my life. I want this baby to know that I love it. Help me, Lord. Amen."

Tilting Maida's head back, Yates sought her lips in a desperate kiss. He needed the reassurance of her love to help him with his struggle. Fear, like a deadly snake, was silent until disturbed. It alone could destroy the relationship that he and Maida had built. And Yates couldn't stand to lose that.

"Are you ready to say goodbye to Reid?" asked Maida.

Yates nodded, regretting the end of their quiet moment together. There was little enough time to spend with his beautiful wife. And although he hadn't wanted to have this conversation, he couldn't deny the feeling of peace that was beginning to wipe away his doubts. He mustered a smile.

"Let's go tell our scapegrace of a son to get going."

Cammie bounced two-year-old Daniel on her hip. His whining and crying only added to her misery. Yet as she watched Treet load the supplies into the wagon, she refused to allow any emotion to show.

Treet was a fine man whom Cammie had grown to love deeply. The only problem was that he wouldn't allow Daniel to come near him. He had seen his own two sons taken from him and sold. On that day he'd sworn never to allow himself to become attached again.

"When you comin' back?" Cammie asked tentatively.

"Don't know, Cammie girl," Treet said nonchalantly.

"One week, two weeks, a month? When?" she prodded.

Setting a bag of flour down, Treet turned to look at Cammie. Her dark skin glistened with perspiration. The boy bouncing on her hip looked too big for her to carry. It was astounding to think that she was the child's mother.

"I'll be back soon as Master Reid is finished delivering the stallion. That's all I know."

"You promise not to let no girl get too friendly with you?"

Treet smiled. "You know you the only girl for me, Cammie." He took Daniel from Cammie's arms and set him on the ground. Wrapping his arms around her, he pulled her close.

Cammie slid her hands up Treet's arms and over his broad shoulders, circling his neck. His skin, a shade darker than hers, was smooth and firm. "You better come back soon, Treet, or I gonna hunt you down."

A chuckle rumbled deep in Treet's chest. "I hear you, girl."

Pulling away, Cammie looked at him. The love in her eyes was like warm honey soothing Treet's scarred heart. She lifted Daniel and walked away without another word.

Watching the sway of her hips, Treet silently groaned. He knew Cammie loved him, but the thought of losing her was more than he could bear. After losing his sons, Treet had vowed never to love another person again. But Cammie had come along with her sweet love talk and turned his head.

He had hoped Cammie would come to him without their being married. But being a Christian, she had refused to go against the Bible's teaching. That meant not lying with him unless they were married. *I wonder what it would be like to be married to her. Would it be such a bad thing?* he wondered. He would have time to think about it on the long journey to Virginia.

Treet wasn't looking forward to the long journey, but at least the young man was good company. Reid Marston, although only fourteen, was delivering a stallion to a respected buyer. Treet was going along to aid and protect the young master. It was a big responsibility for young Reid, but he had proven himself capable since coming to Catawba. He'd worked hard to learn everything he could about horses, and he was now responsible for evaluating the potential of the animals that came to Catawba. Some people had tried to swindle him because he was young, but Reid was knowledgeable beyond his years.

Standing beside the wagon, Treet waited as the family said their goodbyes to the young master. Reid was practically bursting with excitement for the upcoming trip. This was his first opportunity to handle a sale on his own. Previously, Ward had always been in the background while

Reid made the sale, but this time he was completely in charge.

"Make sure you get enough rest and dress warmly in the evenings. I don't want to hear that you were delayed because you got sick," Maida instructed. "Remember your manners and act like a gentleman when you're with others."

"Yes, ma'am." Reid grinned and she looked at him fondly. He was a handsome boy. His boyish good looks made older women want to take care of him like a son and younger women wish he were a little older. His brown hair, cut short, curled riotously around his neck and ears. There was always a sparkle in his pale blue eyes. Reid was smaller than most boys his age, but all of the hard work he'd done around the plantation had strengthened him. He was very proud of his muscles. He didn't mind being shorter than his Uncle Ward, but he was bent on being just as strong.

"I'm proud of you, son." Yates stepped forward, slapping Reid on the shoulder.

"Thank you, Father," Reid's smile broadened. It meant a lot to hear those words. It had been a struggle after coming to Catawba. Ward was training horses and selling lumber, and Yates wanted to plant cotton. Reid knew his father wanted him to follow in his footsteps, but the moment Reid had laid eyes on the horses, his future had been sealed.

"Treet," Yates called up to the black man now seated in the wagon. "You take good care of Reid for us."

"I will, Master Yates."

"Be careful," he warned. "Both of you."

Reid climbed up beside Treet. "We will, Father. Don't worry."

Treet slapped the reins, clicking the horses forward. Reid waved goodbye, turned forward, and laughed out loud. "We're finally on our way, Treet."

"We sure are, Master Reid."

"This is only the first of many adventures to come." Reid was practically bouncing in the seat. In front of others, he was always careful to seem mature and gentlemanly, but when he was alone it didn't matter if he acted like the fourteen year old he was. He couldn't contain himself now.

Treet gave little notice to young Reid as the boy enthusiastically talked on about the trip. He had his mind on his own life. Being away from Cammie was probably for the best, he thought. It would give him a chance to get used to being without her. Since she wanted to be his wife—and Treet was not prepared for that—it was better to be away for awhile. Maybe the longing for Cammie would have lessened by the time he returned.

Laurel stood on the balcony of her room and looked out at Catawba. She could see Reid and Treet pulling away from the barn on their way to Virginia. The beautiful stallion was tied to the back of the wagon. Plans for Reid's trip had begun the day after the party, and he hadn't stopped talking about it since then. Now, a week later, they were finally on their way.

Kendra stood near the split-rail fence talking with a man. Laurel frowned when she saw that it was Joshua Douglas. She didn't know what to make of him. He had flirted outrageously with Marissa during the party last week. But for that brief moment on the veranda, he'd been gentle and considerate toward Laurel. And now here he was spending every day with Kendra. He followed her everywhere.

Not that I'm interested in Joshua Douglas, thought Laurel. *The man can't seem to decide whom he wants to pursue. But he is much too old for Kendra. I must speak with her about this. I don't want to see her hurt by him.*

Now Marissa Ferguson was the one Joshua should be pursuing, Laurel thought wryly. She was closer to his age and had that luscious sort of figure that men couldn't tear their eyes away from. She was definitely more suited for Joshua.

The day after the party, Marissa had ridden over to thank the Marstons for the party. Then she had pulled Laurel up to Laurel's room to talk in private.

"So what did you think of him, Laurel?" Marissa had asked the moment the door was closed. Sitting in a chair across from Laurel, she'd waited expectantly.

"Who?" Laurel had asked, feigning ignorance. She didn't want to have this conversation. Marissa had chuckled.

"You know who I mean, Laurel Marston. You can't fool me. Joshua Douglas, of course."

"Oh him," she'd muttered.

Marissa's eyes had twinkled as she watched Laurel's uncomfortable reaction. It had been entertaining watching Laurel during the party. Her friend had followed Marissa and Joshua's movements all evening. "He's extremely handsome, don't you think?"

Laurel had shrugged, suddenly occupied with making sure her gown was smooth. "I suppose, if you like that type of man."

The poor girl is smitten and doesn't even know it. I wonder what it will take to get a reaction from her, Marissa had smiled to herself. "Joshua Douglas was the most handsome man at the party, and I had his full attention the entire night. I wonder how many of the other girls were eaten up with jealousy."

It hadn't been easy for Laurel to sit and listen while Marissa talked about girls and envy of Joshua. Especially when Laurel was one of them. She'd hated herself for admitting it, but Marissa didn't need to know.

"I've got a secret to tell you, Laurel," Marissa had whispered, leaning forward conspiratorially. "Joshua Douglas kissed me."

"What!" Laurel's surprise had been more for the fact that Marissa was confiding in her. Although they were friends, there had been few shared confidences. Their conversations were usually limited to fashion and beauty secrets.

This is perfect, Marissa had thought, watching Laurel's reaction. *What would little Laurel do if she knew the truth about that evening.*

The moment Marissa had seen Laurel step out to the veranda that night, Marissa had known what she needed to do. It was the perfect chance to irritate Laurel using Joshua Douglas. Suggestively, she had asked Joshua to take her outside for a breath of fresh air. He had complied immediately.

It hadn't been easy finding Laurel in the dark, but Marissa had caught a glimpse of her gown behind the pillar. Guiding Joshua toward her, she had manipulated the entire situation. The conversation couldn't have gone any better, and Joshua had played his part to perfection.

"Do you love him?"

Laurel's question had shaken Marissa from her reverie. "Love him? Why, no."

"Then how could you allow him to kiss you?"

Marissa had been unable to keep from laughing as she stood up. "Laurel, you're such a child sometimes. You don't have to love a man just to enjoy a kiss."

"But that's not proper!" Laurel couldn't believe Marissa's attitude. She had been taught that a proper lady never let a gentleman take such privileges. A brief kiss was allowed between betrothed, but no more.

"Who cares?" Marissa had shrugged. "Men enjoy kissing me, and most of the time I enjoy it too."

"But what about your husband?"

Marissa had frowned at Laurel's prudish attitude. "My husband will appreciate the knowledge I have after we're married. Men want a virgin for their bride, but not an ignorant one."

"How do you know?" Marissa had shrugged again. "But how can they respect you if you're so . . . so loose?"

"Men don't respect women," Marissa had answered in disgust. "They may act like they do before marriage, but afterward you're more like a slave."

"That's not true, Marissa. My father and Uncle Ward love and respect their wives," Laurel had said defensively, standing up.

Marissa had snorted. "I don't know about your father, but I could tell you some things about your Uncle Ward."

Laurel had been shocked. "What are you talking about?"

With a toss of her hand, Marissa had turned away. "It doesn't matter. I'd better be off now. Do you wish to walk me down?"

Numbly, Laurel had nodded and followed Marissa from the room. *What did she mean about Uncle Ward? He* does *love and respect Aunt Taylor. I've seen the way he treats her. What is Marissa talking about?*

Marissa had sensed the turmoil her words were causing. Waiting until they were outside and no one was around, she had proceeded. With as much uncertainty as she could muster, she had stopped Laurel. "If I tell you, can you keep this a secret?"

"Yes."

Wringing her hands a little for effect, Marissa had said, "Your Uncle Ward has been spending a lot of time with me lately." She'd paused and taken a deep breath. "The other day he came close to kissing me."

"What?" Laurel had practically shouted.

"Shhh," Marissa had hissed, glancing around to see if anyone was listening. "You promised to keep this a secret, Laurel. You're my dearest friend, and I would hate to hurt anyone by causing problems. I'm not going to be coming around as often so that your uncle isn't tempted to do something he'd regret later. Do you understand what I'm saying?"

"Yes," Laurel had whispered hoarsely.

"Are you all right, Laurel? You seem awfully pale."

"I'm fine."

"Why don't you go back into the house. I'll see you later."

Marissa had hugged Laurel close and left. Stunned by her insinuations, Laurel had gone back to her room and laid on her bed, staring at the ceiling. Could what she said about Uncle Ward be true? What about love and respect? Would Jason respect her after they were married?

Laurel's head still reeled with these questions a week later. She had watched Ward closely, hoping to see an indication of what Marissa had implied. There had been nothing. Of course, Marissa hadn't been around since that day.

The only one visiting all week was Joshua Douglas.

Laurel had tried to be polite to Mr. Douglas when he had first come to visit, but the man refused to acknowledge her. He talked and laughed with Kendra, but wouldn't even recognize Laurel. She had hoped that without Marissa Ferguson around to distract him, Joshua would at least notice her. Did the man think that she was too plain to look at? Was Kendra prettier?

Jealous? Me, jealous over that man? Absolutely not! Laurel argued with herself. *If he wants to spend so much time with Kendra, that's fine with me. My Jason is coming soon, and he'll be all the man I need.* Strangely, though, even the thought of Jason Portland couldn't excite Laurel.

I just don't like to be snubbed by such a handsome man, she reasoned. *If he would pay me just one compliment, I wouldn't give him another thought.* Of course, she would have to spend time around him if she wanted that compliment. That would not be easy. But it was a small price to pay to erase him from her thoughts.

Laurel closed the French doors with a snap as she reentered her bedroom. Her rose-colored day dress swished around her ankles as she marched purposefully down the stairs and outside. This was a challenge she was determined to meet head-on—and win.

With her brightest smile, Laurel greeted her sister and their visitor. "Hello, Kendra. Mr. Douglas."

"Hi, Laurel," Kendra said distractedly.

Joshua bowed slightly at the waist. "Good afternoon, Miss Marston."

Laurel frowned as Joshua turned his back on her to give his full attention to the horse in the center ring. Pursing her lips in determination, she watched the horse. Pickle stood in the middle of the ring, holding a lead rope to one of the mares. He flicked a small whip to give the horse instructions.

After a few moments, Pickle led the horse toward them. Stopping in front of Laurel he smiled warmly. "Afternoon, Missy Laurel. How you doin' this fine day?"

"I'm doing quite well, Pickle. And you?"

"Just dandy." Pickle turned to Joshua. "What you think, Master Douglas? Fine horse, ain't she?"

"She certainly is."

Pickle's weathered skin stretched into another smile. "Oh, by the way, Missy Laurel, I want to make sure you 'member we goin' out in the mornin'."

Laurel eagerly leaned against the split railing, not caring if she got her gown dirty. "I remember. I've got everything prepared. What time are we heading out?"

Pickle's dark skin furrowed into a frown. "Daybreak, I think would be best. I got a lot to show you."

Tomorrow was her and Pickle's day to spend in the swamp. No one in the family understood Laurel's love for the swamp. It had happened so gradually that she was surprised by it herself. Pickle had wanted to show her how to survive in the swamp if she ever became stranded. True, asking Yates Marston for permission to go into the swamp with Pickle had been difficult. Even though Pickle was a free man, Yates continued to view him as a slave. But concern for his daughter's safety finally convinced him. The swamp was indeed deadly. Knowing how miserable Laurel had been about moving to South Carolina, Yates had hoped learning about the swamp would help her adjust to their adopted country.

It had. Laurel took to the swamp eagerly. Now she and Pickle would go as many as three days a week. But this trip, which they had been planning for many weeks, was to be an overnight.

"I'll be ready, don't worry," Laurel said.

"Okay, Missy Laurel, I see you in the mornin'."

Laurel's eyes lighted with excitement. She hadn't been able to spend any time in the swamp since the party. It would do her good to get away from the plantation for a while. Maybe she would be able to sort through the things Marissa had said. Laurel always seemed to think more clearly out in her beloved swamp.

"Excuse me, Miss Marston," Joshua's voice interrupted her musings. "If you don't mind my asking—where are you going with that slave tomorrow?"

Laurel's blue eyes glittered. Wouldn't he be shocked by her answer! "Pickle is not a slave, Mr. Douglas. He's a free man."

Joshua's jaw clenched briefly before he apologized. "I'm sorry for my mistake, Miss Marston. I meant no offense."

"That's quite all right, Mr. Douglas. To answer your question, Pickle and I are going into the swamp."

"The swamp?" he asked in disbelief.

"Yes, the swamp." Laurel lifted her chin defiantly.

"I see."

Laurel glared at Joshua. His tone was insulting. Even the look in his eyes, although they were beautiful deep-blue eyes, was condescending. With Marissa's words about men's lack of respect for women so fresh in her mind, Laurel decided to give Joshua Douglas a piece of her mind.

"Mr. Douglas, women were not created merely to sit around the house sipping tea, sewing, and having children. We can do things just as well as men, if given the opportunity. And I don't appreciate you insinuating that we can't."

Bowing slightly at the waist, a teasing glint in his eye, Joshua's voice softened. "Once again, I apologize to you, Miss Marston. It seems I have erred in my judgment of many things. I promise it won't happen again."

Laurel sensed that there was more to his words than a simple apology, but before she could pursue it further, Musket began barking. Kendra, Joshua, and Laurel all turned to see a lone rider coming down the lane toward them. He pulled to a stop in front of them and dismounted.

"May I help you, sir?" Laurel asked.

"If you could direct me to a Miss Laurel Marston, please, I would appreciate it." A scruffy beard and mustache completely hid the man's mouth from sight as he squinted at Laurel.

Laurel nodded her head in acknowledgment. "I am Miss Marston. What do you want of me?"

Sliding a hand inside his vest, the man extracted a large envelope from the waist of his breeches. "I was asked to deliver this to you, miss."

Reaching for the envelope, Laurel's heart stopped for a moment. Could it be that Jason had already arrived? Her nervous fingers extracted the letter. Reading it quickly, she found that the Portlands had indeed arrived but would not be coming to Catawba for several days. It seemed the voyage had been rough, and both Clair and Jason needed to recover.

"Thank you, sir. You have brought good news." She pointed in the direction of the well. "Please refresh yourself." With a grateful nod, the man led his horse away.

"Is it from the Portlands?" asked Kendra.

"Yes. They'll be here sometime next week." Scanning the letter again, Laurel tried to find any clue that Jason was coming to ask for her hand in marriage.

"Are you still going out tomorrow?"

Laurel considered. If Jason wasn't coming until next week, she had plenty of time. She and Pickle would only be gone for one day and night. Laurel nodded emphatically. "Yes, I'll still be leaving tomorrow."

"I hope no harm comes to you out in the wilds of the swamp, Miss Marston," Joshua said mockingly.

Laurel glared at him. "It's none of your concern whether harm comes to me or not, Mr. Douglas." Turning on her heel, Laurel marched away as Kendra gaped in surprise.

"I apologize for my sister's rudeness, Mr. Douglas. I have no idea why she spoke like that." As a matter of fact, Kendra didn't understand a lot of what Laurel did anymore. They had never been close, but since coming to Catawba, Laurel had changed. She was no longer the whiny, spoiled girl she had been when they arrived at Catawba. Kendra was unsure how to act around her sister anymore.

"Quite all right, Miss Marston. I think I deserved it." A puzzled frown creased Joshua's brow. "Where does Pickle take her when they go into the swamp?" he inquired.

"I'm not sure. They leave at sunrise and come back well after dark. Laurel never talks about her trips."

"What does she do out there?"

"You'd have to ask Pickle." Kendra watched Joshua's face closely at the mention of Pickle's name, hoping to see a reaction.

"No, I think I'll have to find out on my own," Joshua muttered to himself. Miss Laurel Marston had captured his attention just now. Finding out that the proper young lady had shot a man while protecting her family was interesting, but hearing that she spent time in the swamp was very intriguing indeed.

Joshua began formulating a plan in his mind. It would be enjoyable to see what made the beautiful Laurel Marston tick. Was it possible he'd misjudged her at their first meeting?

Court stood at the edge of the trees watching Kendra. Her waist-length brown hair was braided straight down her back. She was wearing one of Court's favorite gowns, and she looked beautiful as she stood beside Joshua Douglas.

Court and Kendra had had no time alone since their meeting several weeks ago, just before the big party. No stolen glances or smiles had come Court's way even when he worked near her the past few days. He had noticed that Kendra was spending a great deal of time with Joshua Douglas, and he didn't know what to think. Could it be that his Kendra was falling in love with another man?

Court's insides began to gnaw at him and he returned to his work with a vengeance. There was nothing he could do until she came to him.

Laurel tiptoed down the hall to the stairs, peeking around the corner to make sure none of the servants were around. Seeing no one, she hurried down the stairs, dashing out the front door and down to the barn. Pickle was waiting for her. Smiling, he greeted her, ignoring the unladylike display that she had just made by running. Laurel's lectures to Kendra about racing around Catawba would lose their impact if Kendra ever saw her big sister running.

"Morning, Missy Laurel."

"Good morning, Pickle," Laurel gasped, trying to catch her breath.

"You ready to go?"

"Definitely." Instead of her usual ladylike gown, Laurel wore a riding habit that had been altered drastically. It consisted of a loosened corset, which made their long walks possible, a loose-fitting riding coat which she wore over her fine linen shirt, and a riding skirt that had been cut and altered to fit close to each leg, almost like trousers. Laurel was able to walk, climb, and even run without being hindered by her clothing. She knew Yates would have forbidden her to wear such an outrageous outfit if he'd known about it, but she'd been successful in keeping it from him. The pack slung across her back contained a gown that fit perfectly over the riding habit. She would return to Catawba wearing the gown.

"Let's go, then." Pickle slung a pack onto his back and walked toward the trees. This was his territory. He'd learned how to survive in the swamp during the Revolutionary War.

"What are we going to learn today, Pickle?"

"It's time to learn a little trappin'. If'n you get into the wilds without a gun to shoot, you have to know how to trap. I'll teach you how to track an animal, set a trap, and kill without a weapon."

Laurel turned a little pale at the thought of killing an animal with her bare hands. She didn't like the idea. "Pickle, are you sure I need to learn that?" she asked.

"I think so."

"Very well," Laurel surrendered. She knew Pickle had her best interests in mind.

Only moments after entering the woods, Pickle froze in his tracks. Laurel had learned long ago to do whatever he did, so she also stopped. Not moving a muscle, she strained to hear. Was something out there?

Pickle's head moved from left to right. Lowering his head, he closed his eyes and listened intently.

After a moment, Laurel whispered, "What is it, Pickle? Do you hear something?"

"Someone be followin' us, Missy Laurel," Pickle stated calmly.

"Who could be following us?"

"I don't know, but we best be careful." With that they continued their progress through the woods.

A few minutes later Laurel asked, "Do you think they're still there?" Perspiration trickled down her back. She wiped the sweat from her face.

"Yeah. Gettin' easier to hear."

Laurel looked around carefully, trying to see if anything was out of the ordinary. Thick trees rose proudly toward the sky. Overgrown bushes made walking difficult. The air smelled musty and wet. The closer they got to the swamp the more moisture hung in the air. Laurel couldn't take deep breaths because of its thickness.

The sounds of the swamp were extraordinary. If she listened closely, she could almost hear a snake creeping along the ground. The denseness of the forest calmed her. Laurel knew that was why she loved the swamp. It didn't matter if she acted like a lady or not; the swamp would accept her as long as she could survive in it.

Swatting away the mosquitoes that persisted in feeding on her skin, Laurel glanced around. They were almost to the swamp. The ground was already showing signs of wetness.

The sudden snap of a twig directly behind Laurel pulled her and Pickle up short. Dropping to the ground, Pickle soundlessly crept toward the noise. Laurel remained still. She quickly prayed for Pickle's safety.

Behind her, Pickle angled toward the sound. The scent of a man reached his nostrils. Time in the woods was the only way to get rid of the smell, and they hadn't been walking long enough.

Easing forward a few more feet, he spotted a dark figure hunched over near a large tree with his back to him. Silently

Pickle stood and took a step forward, pulling his large knife from the sheath.

Placing the knife tip to the man's throat, Pickle growled, "Don't move or I slice you up and leave you for the animals to eat." The man froze. "Now turn 'round slow like."

Pickle took a step back as the man twisted around. "Well, well, well. What do we have here?" He slipped his knife back into its sheath. "I don't suppose you gonna tell ole Pickle what you doin' here."

"No, I don't suppose I'm going to," Joshua Douglas said good naturedly.

Pickle jerked his head back toward Laurel and said, "You come to join us. You gonna have to stay with us now."

Joshua didn't say anything as Pickle turned and retraced his steps. "It's all right, Missy Laurel," the old servant called.

Laurel got to her feet when she heard Pickle's words. As he walked into the small clearing, she was smiling in relief. The smile melted the second she caught sight of the man behind him.

Joshua Douglas! "What are you doing here?" she snapped.

Joshua sauntered into the clearing and sat down. "I wanted to see what this old man was going to teach you. Since none of your family seemed to know, my curiosity got the better of me."

"You followed us?" Laurel asked in dismay.

"I guess I did. You're stuck with me," Joshua replied, stretching his legs out and slanting a glance up at her. Laurel Marston was a beauty—of that there was no doubt. But to see her standing there, hands on her hips, eyes sparkling with anger, was enough to bring a man to his knees. She was the image of every man's dreams—at least his dreams, Joshua was surprised to find himself thinking.

Determination burned in Laurel's eyes. *How dare he follow us?* she thought. Then she stiffened. *Will he tell Father what he's seen?* Glancing down at her outfit, flames of embarrassment shot up her neck and cheeks. No one had ever seen her swamp apparel except Pickle. The altered skirt was so daring. What would Joshua think?

Turning her back quickly, Laurel picked up her pack. "Are we going to sit here all day, Pickle? Let's go." Chin high, she walked away from the men.

Pickle shook his head. "You sure do know how to get 'em riled." Chuckling, he got up and followed Laurel.

Joshua only smiled, and stood to follow Pickle. He had spent the previous evening wondering what would entice Laurel Marston to go into the swamp. He'd done enough tracking himself to know that it was deadly and very few people survived in it. But she came to them willingly and with what appeared to Joshua as excitement.

He couldn't remember the moment he'd decided to follow Laurel and Pickle, but before anyone else was awake and moving around his farm, he was up and dressed. He knew he'd have to be watching for Laurel and Pickle in order to follow them. It was a good thing Kendra had known when they usually left.

Joshua had followed close behind the pair for a while, wanting to make sure Laurel would be safe with Pickle; he wasn't quite sure what to think of a young lady alone with a freed slave. To have the old man sneak up on him had been embarrassing. He couldn't remember the last time someone had gotten the drop on him like that.

Laurel was angrily wondering why Joshua had followed her. She tried to think of a plausible explanation but had no answer. Unless he had merely decided to spend a day harassing—he seemed quite good at that. Which brought her to the look she had seen in his eyes a moment ago. Could it have been interest? Did Joshua Douglas find her appealing after all? Laurel thought it was fascination that had glimmered in those blue eyes. But why? After all the time he'd spent snubbing her, why did he seem intrigued now?

And what about Kendra? Would he choose me over her? Laurel scolded herself for such awful thoughts. Kendra was her sister. She didn't deserve to lose Joshua if she really wanted him. *But if he chooses me, who am I to say no?*

Laurel knew she was being fanciful. It had hurt to have Joshua Douglas, a handsome, virile man, show no interest whatsoever in her. She tried to tell herself it didn't matter what he thought of her. As long as Jason liked her, nothing else mattered. *There's probably a good explanation for his following us*, Laurel thought. *But what?*

"Watch where you goin', girl," bellowed Pickle.

Laurel suddenly realized she was in the midst of marshy land. This was one of the most dangerous parts of the swamp; a person could stand on the thick mud without noticing she was sinking until it was too late.

"Sorry, Pickle," mumbled Laurel.

Pulling Laurel behind him, Pickle took the lead. "Don't want nuthin' to happen to you."

Hanging her head, Laurel refused to meet Joshua's mocking glance. She silently followed Pickle further into the swamp.

Lizy sat on the bed in the corner of the room. The saferoom, the man named Court called it. He was here now with a woman named Miss Taylor. Lizy thought she had never seen anyone as beautiful as Miss Taylor. She was delicate and soft and clean and all the things that Lizy had never been in her entire short life. Miss Taylor was talking to her now.

"Lizy, I know you're afraid, but we need you to talk to us. Unless you let us know who you belong to—who beat you—we won't be able to help you stay away from him. Do you understand?" Taylor paused, waiting for Lizy to acknowledge her. Lizy only stared with great, dark eyes.

Taylor sighed. They had been at this for close to an hour and had yet to get a response from the frightened little girl.

"Lizy, please tell us," she said gently. "We promise we won't take you back to him." After another silence, she looked over at Court. "It's no use. She's not going to tell us anything."

Court, who had been leaning against the wall of the tiny room, jerked erect in exasperation. At his movement, Lizy gasped and cringed reflexively, curling herself into an even smaller ball. Court froze.

"I'm sorry, Lizy. I didn't mean to scare you. You should know you're safe with us." He smiled. "Besides, I've already felt your kicks and knocks, remember? I'm not likely to try my luck against you again. I don't need any more bruises."

At Court's teasing remark, Lizy relaxed a fraction, even allowed herself a tiny, hesitant smile. She liked the tall man with his fiery head of hair. He had checked on her twice before, bringing candles to light the dark.

Court was encouraged by her reaction. He crossed to sit beside her. "Where did you learn to fight like that anyway?"

Taylor held her breath, praying that the girl would respond. After a moment's silence, she was rewarded.

"I gots brothers 'n' sisters," Lizy whispered. "We always fightin'."

"Really?" Court said. "How many brothers and sisters? I never had any myself."

Lizy was surprised. She couldn't imagine not having siblings. "I gots two brothers 'n' two sisters." Pride made her add, "I'm the next oldest one." Then, as if dismayed at her outburst, she retreated into her shell.

Taylor stepped forward. "Lizy, you must miss your family very much. I'm sure you're worried about them. Do they get beaten too?"

Lizy looked at Taylor with tortured eyes, thinking of her family. She had no idea if they were all right or if they were being punished because she'd run away. She hated to think that they might be beaten because of her. But she'd had to leave. She couldn't stay, knowing that the overseer would come for her. Surely her family would understand. Closing her eyes, Lizy laid her head on her crossed arms.

Taylor tried once more. "Lizy, are you owned by Joshua Douglas? Is he the one who beat you?" But Lizy, lost in her own misery, refused to answer.

With a despairing glance at each other, Taylor and Court climbed from the room and closed the door, leaving the young girl in silence and candlelight.

Laurel was ready to scream in frustration. They had been in the swamp for several hours, and she may as well have been there for the first time. She was clumsy and distracted, and nothing Pickle had asked her to do was going right.

Dragging several fronds together, Laurel began laying them evenly across the ground. Limbs for the shelter were next. She had to venture further into the dense growth for those. Through the thick, leafy branches, the early afternoon sun beat down on her unprotected head. Although she loved the swamp, the filth of trekking through it made the enjoyment two-edged. By the time she finished, perspiration was rolling down her face and neck and trickling down between her shoulder blades.

"You all right, Missy Laurel?" Pickle asked

"I'm fine," Laurel huffed in exhaustion. Wearily she swatted away the bugs that buzzed around her head.

"You don't look fine."

"Thanks a lot," Laurel muttered.

Glancing at Joshua, Laurel frowned as she saw that he was watching her intently. Heat and frustration added sting to her words. "If you are going to eat our food and share our shelter, Mr. Douglas, I suggest that you get up and help. You'll not be waited on by us."

"Now wait a minute, Missy Laurel. I gonna teach you how to track and trap. Why don't we let this young fella just rest?"

"That's all right, Pickle. I'll get my own food. I want to make sure we have something to eat tonight." With a insolent smile, Joshua stood and stretched briefly before turning to leave the clearing.

"And just what do you mean by that?" Laurel screeched at Joshua's retreating back. She couldn't believe what she'd just heard. The man was impossible. If it weren't for him she'd be enjoying her time in the swamp.

Turning slowly, Joshua gave her a hard stare. "It means I don't want to go hungry tonight if you're the one responsible for feeding us. To trap an animal, you have to have cunning and patience. I don't think you can do it, Miss Marston."

Laurel took a deep breath and silently counted to ten before answering his insult. "Well, Mr. Douglas, I think you're wrong. Would you care to make a small wager on the matter?"

"What type of wager are you talking about, Miss Marston?" Joshua asked, lifting his brow.

Laurel stood her ground, hands planted on her hips. She was determined to make this man eat his words. "I'll spend the day with Pickle showing me the basics of tracking and trapping. After we return, you and I will go our separate ways to hunt for the evening meal. Each of us will have two hours—whatever we have at the end of that time we bring back. The one who brings back the most wins."

"Wins what?" Joshua asked calmly.

"What would you want?" she asked boldly.

Looking down at her, a wicked grin spread slowly across his tan features. Laurel swallowed hard. "Oh, I'll think of something."

"Very well," she replied faintly.

"And if, by some miracle, *you* win—what do you want, Miss Marston?"

Stubbornly she lifted her chin. "I want you to pay me a compliment." *I'll get my compliment from him one way or another,* she thought.

"A compliment? That's all you want?" Joshua was puzzled. He hadn't expected that.

"That's all."

Shrugging a shoulder, Joshua walked up to Laurel and held out his hand. "You've got yourself a bet, Miss Marston."

Laurel looked from his hand to his face. She knew he didn't think she was capable of winning, but tenacity was one of Laurel's strong points. Clasping his hand firmly, she shook it and smiled. "I'll see you after my lessons."

"In the meantime, I'll see if I can rustle up a snack. If you'll excuse me, Miss Marston. Pickle." With a mock salute, Joshua left the clearing and was instantly swallowed from view.

Suddenly nervous, Laurel craned her neck to catch a glimpse of him. She hoped he knew what he was doing out here. It just wouldn't do if Joshua got hurt or killed while hunting for food.

Pickle scratched his weathered cheek. "I don't know what that be all 'bout, Missy Laurel, but if'n you wants to win, we best get goin'."

"I'm going to beat that man if it's the last thing I do," Laurel muttered to herself. She'd have her compliment and forget about Joshua Douglas. If she could. Was it possible to ignore such a powerful man? Did she really want to?

"You like that young fella, don't you, Missy Laurel?" There was no question in Pickle's voice, only a matter-of-fact statement.

"I don't know what you mean," Laurel retorted, her cheeks flushing pinkly.

"Aah, now don't go an' lie to old Pickle. My eyes may be old, but they not blind."

Laurel's eyes widened. "Pickle, please," she whispered.

"Don't get upset, girl. If you worried 'bout it, I don't think that boy sees it."

Laurel couldn't help but sigh. Pickle was her dear friend. She didn't mind his knowing she was interested in Joshua Douglas. But Laurel prayed no one else could see it. She hoped it wasn't that obvious.

Maida smiled at her reflection. Turning sideways, she smoothed her hand down her belly, smiling when she saw the bulge. It was still small. She wondered how much longer it would be before others would notice.

Sitting down in a chair by the large windows, she picked up the tiny muslin gown she was stitching for the baby. Tenderly she stroked the material against her cheek, thinking of the day she would hold her child and feel the baby's smooth skin against hers. She hummed a soft lullaby as she returned to her stitching.

She was interrupted by a knock on the door and Taylor's soft voice. "Maida, are you busy?" Taylor asked as she stepped into the room.

Maida happily jumped from her seat, thrusting the small gown in front of Taylor's face. "I'm working on an outfit for the baby. Isn't it adorable?"

Taylor stiffened, pasting a smile on her face. "Lovely. I didn't mean to interrupt you. Excuse me." She turned quickly from the room, leaving an open-mouthed Maida in surprise.

Taylor had carefully avoided Maida since her announcement. The less she had to hear about Maida's pregnancy, the better. *Stop feeling sorry for yourself,* she berated herself. *You should be happy for Maida, not jealous. Just because you haven't given Ward a child doesn't mean everyone else should be barren.*

Taylor hated feeling jealous of Maida. She wanted to be happy for her friend, but it wasn't easy. The desire to give Ward a child of his own consumed her. Brooke might call Ward Daddy, but she wasn't really his. Ward had never mentioned having children, but what father doesn't want a son to take his place?

Taylor felt like a failure. Maybe it would be better if Ward *were* married to Marissa Ferguson. She was young and healthy. Surely it would be easy for her to have children.

She frowned bitterly at the thought of the young vixen. Marissa had been at Catawba this morning. Ostensibly there to visit Laurel, she had managed to corner Ward in the yard. They had spent the time discussing his favorite stallion, which Marissa was quick to admire. As Taylor passed by at one point, the girl had had her hand on Ward's arm, earnestly looking into his face. Taylor was certain she had seen Marissa smirk as she felt Taylor's glance.

She slipped into her bedroom, hoping for a moment alone to deal with her feelings of self-pity. But before she could sit down there was a knock on the door. With a sigh she went to open it.

"Taylor, are you all right?" Maida asked in concern.

"I'm fine," Taylor said calmly.

"There must be something. It's not just this. You've been avoiding me since before the party. If I walk into a room, you walk out. If I'm in the parlor, you're in the garden or on the porch or anywhere I'm not. Have I done something to hurt you?"

Taylor hesitated. How could she tell Maida that her pregnancy was the problem? It had nothing to do with her personally, but the baby she now carried.

"I'm not leaving until you tell me what it is," Maida continued. Sitting down in a chair by the fireplace, she crossed her arms and waited.

"It's nothing."

"What would you do if I had a problem and didn't feel like talking?" Maida asked

"I'd try to help you," Taylor admitted.

"Exactly." Maida perched on the edge of the chair. "You're always helping others. Why won't you let someone help you?"

Tears pricked Taylor's eyes. Clasping her hands together, she sat down across from Maida. "It's not that I don't want help, but there's nothing you can do."

"Will you tell me why you look so sad?"

Taylor shook her head, unsure whether she could talk around the lump in her throat. *I want to give my husband a child. I'm tired of waiting. I can't help being jealous of you, Maida,* she screamed inside, but she maintained her calm facade.

Maida leaned back, watching Taylor. "I can see it in your eyes, Taylor. If you won't tell me I'll speak with Ward and ask him to find out what it is," she threatened.

"You wouldn't."

"Yes, I would. Whatever it is, it's eating you up inside. You can't let it continue."

Taylor considered this. Ward wouldn't understand how she felt. He would say Brooke was the only child they needed, even though she was from Taylor's first marriage.

"I don't want to talk about it, Maida. Trust me. It's something I need to deal with by myself," she pleaded.

"Why won't you let me help?"

"Because it's selfish of me, and I don't want anyone to know how I feel." Rising, Taylor left the room without another word. She needed to pray. *What is more selfish than resenting a friend because she's pregnant?* she thought miserably. It had taken five years for her to conceive with her first husband. With Ward, Taylor had hoped it wouldn't be so long, but her hopes were quickly diminishing.

Her thoughts turned inward, Taylor failed to notice the men standing at the bottom of the porch steps. "Excuse us, ma'am," one called, startling her from her musings.

"Can I help you gentlemen?"

Taylor assumed the one speaking was the leader of the three men standing before her. As he pulled his hat off, long dirty hair fell limply around his face. A bushy beard and mustache dwarfed his small head. There didn't appear to be a clean spot on his entire body.

"My name's Pete. This here's Joe and Sam," he motioned to the two men beside him. "We was wonderin' if there's a young girl here with long brown hair that rides a dark little mare."

"Why do you want to know?" Taylor asked sternly.

"We just want to ask her some questions, ma'am."

"What kind of questions?"

Pete's eyes squinted up at Taylor. "We're lookin' for a runaway slave girl. The girl we lookin' for ran into the young lady. We haven't been able to find the runaway, so we was wantin' to ask the young lady if she could tell us anythin' more about her."

Fear froze Taylor the instant the man mentioned Lizy. Did he suspect they were hiding the girl right here at Catawba? The man named Pete was watching her closely. She hoped he couldn't see that she was afraid. Clasping her hands in front of her, she answered as calmly as she could, "Who does this slave girl belong to?"

"It don't matter. She's a runaway."

Taylor needed to get information from this man. If he could tell her who owned Lizy, then they wouldn't have to spy on Joshua Douglas any longer. "But how do you know to whom you return her once she's caught?"

"Don't go worryin' your pretty head 'bout that, ma'am. We always return 'em to their masters. Now, 'bout the young lady we're lookin' for. Does she live here?"

"I believe you're speaking of my niece."

Pete instantly straightened, eyes glittering sharply. "Could we talk to her, ma'am?"

"Of course. I'll see if she's here." She motioned across the yard. "If you gentlemen would care for a drink, the well is just over there."

"Thank you, ma'am," Pete said, slapping his hat back onto his head. The three men turned and walked back toward the well.

Taylor, taking a deep breath, retreated to the house. Cammie was waiting.

"Miss Kendra is in her room."

"Thank you, Cammie." The tightness in her throat made speaking difficult. Trying to calm herself, she went upstairs to Kendra's room and stepped in with a knock. "Kendra."

Kendra looked up from where she was reading by the window and, seeing Taylor's pale features, quickly stood. "Aunt Taylor, what's wrong?" She crossed the room and led Taylor to a chair, then seated herself opposite her aunt. "What's wrong? Is it Lizy?"

The little runaway was still hidden in the secret room. They hadn't liked leaving her there for so long, but her frail body was healing from her beatings. Lizy had steadfastly refused to say a word about her master.

"No, it's not Lizy," said Taylor, shaking her head. "At least, not exactly."

"Then what's wrong? You look ready to faint."

"There are three men downstairs that want to talk to you." Kendra gasped. "I believe they're the ones that you ran into when you were in the woods with Lizy." Taylor closed her eyes. She was frightened. Helping runaways had never been easy, but she had never come this close to being caught.

Kendra fell from her chair and knelt in front of Taylor, clutching her hands tightly. "What are we going to do?" she whispered. "What do they want? Do they know we have Lizy? Will they take her back?"

As the questions rolled out, Kendra's eyes grew large with fear. Taylor saw in Kendra the mirror image of what she felt herself. *Oh, Father, help us*, she whispered silently. *What are we going to do?* She fought to control her anxiety.

It was then that a scripture verse began to repeat itself over and over in her mind. *"Fear thou not; for I am with thee. . . . Fear thou not; for I am with thee. . . ."* Closing her eyes, she let the words wash over her as Kendra knelt before her. Then she nodded.

"Listen to me, Kendra." A new light of determination flashed in her eyes. "We don't have to be afraid. Remember, we have God on our side. We can't let these men frighten us into telling them anything."

"But what if they already know we have Lizy?" Kendra frantically searched Taylor's face. It was serene.

"Let's pray before we do anything else." Bowing her head, Taylor began. "Father God, the Bible says we don't have to be afraid—you are with us. Let your peace fill Kendra right now, so she won't be afraid anymore. Show us what we need to do and say to these men to get them away from here. Above all, Lord, protect Lizy. Lead us to the right path to best help this little girl. In your son's name, amen."

Kendra sat quietly with Taylor for a moment before speaking. "I'm ready to talk to them, Aunt Taylor."

Proud of her niece's strength, Taylor stood. "Very well. Let's go together."

The three men stood waiting for them. As Kendra and Taylor stepped onto the porch together, they pulled off their hats.

"You're the one," Pete stated, pointing at Kendra.

"I'm the one what?" Kendra asked boldly.

"You're the gal that told us where to go after the runaway. We've been lookin' for her nigh on a week and there's been no sign of her."

"So what do you want from me?"

"My guess is you helped that slave and she's hidin' somewhere 'round here." Pete's filthy finger pointed accusingly at Kendra.

Kendra threw back her head and laughed, causing the men to look at one another in confusion. "Do you honestly think I would risk death by helping a runaway? I can assure you, sir, I have no wish to die for anyone."

Pete scratched at his beard, nonplussed. He'd hoped to show up here and scare the young lady into telling him where the girl was. He had little doubt that she'd helped the runaway. Otherwise he and his men would have found her by now. They were some of the best runaway trackers.

"Then I suppose you wouldn't mind it if we took a look around the place," Pete suggested slyly. He turned as if to do just that.

Taylor spoke up boldly.

"Excuse me, sir, but I think I would mind. If you wish to search the plantation, then you will have to wait until my husband returns. He alone can grant you permission, and he isn't here right now."

"Well, when will he be back?" Pete snapped.

"Just before sundown."

"That won't be for another six hours," he snarled.

Taylor only shrugged. "If you wish to look around, then you will have to wait until then. The choice is up to you."

Slamming his hat back on his head, Pete glared up at the two finely dressed women. "I'll be back. And when I do, you won't be able to stop me from lookin' around." Turning, he gestured toward the others and they left.

Taylor and Kendra breathed a sigh of relief in unison. "That was close, Aunt Taylor."

"Yes." She smiled. "But God was with us."

Kendra nodded. "What will you do when Uncle Ward comes home and those men ask him to look around?"

"I don't know. We'll have to wait and see."

"Does Uncle Ward know what you do?" Kendra asked.

"Yes."

"Will he be upset about these men coming?"

"He'll handle them just fine. They can look around all they want, but they'll never find the room."

Taylor looked off across the plantation, her heart fluttering at the thought of telling Ward about the men. He knew about Taylor helping the runaways, but he never knew when they had one staying in the saferoom. He and Court had worked together in the evenings, digging the hole under the barn. They even designed the heavy trapdoor to sound like the rest of the floor if anyone stomped on it.

After the room was finished, Taylor had insisted that Ward not be involved with the runaways. She wanted to protect him, and if anything should ever happen to her, she wanted Ward to take care of Brooke. They'd had several arguments during their marriage, but none of them came close to the one they'd had when Taylor had made that announcement.

"Do you think they'll come back?"

"There's no doubt about it," said Taylor.

With a heavy sigh, Kendra dropped her head. She didn't know if she had the strength to face those men and their accusations again. She felt completely drained. Taylor, sensing Kendra's despair, wrapped a comforting arm around her shoulder.

"It'll be all right, Kendra. Don't let those men frighten you."

"I'll try not to, Aunt Taylor. This is just so new to me; it's a little scary."

"I know, honey. Why don't you go for a ride. Maybe that will help revive you."

"Thanks, Aunt Taylor. That's a great idea." Hugging Taylor, Kendra ran inside to change. A ride was just what she needed. During breakfast, she'd heard Ward discussing the work that was being done and Court's name had been mentioned. She didn't know the exact location, but she had a rough idea of where she could find him.

Moments later, racing Turnip toward the woods, Kendra felt much better. The farther she rode, the more she let the tension from those men and their questions roll away. An entire week spent with Joshua Douglas, trying to find out the truth about Lizy, had also weighed heavily on her mind. Kendra let it go. She was going to find Court and he would make her feel better. In anticipation, she spurred her mount on, for once ignoring the beautiful day and the animals that scurried into hiding at the sound of thundering hooves.

The echoing ring of an ax told Kendra that she had ridden in the right direction. She followed the sound, careful not to get too close, and saw a couple of men chopping trees. Court was not among them.

She moved Turnip further into the woods, listening for the sound of another ax. Silence. She finally stopped and slid from the saddle, her hands unconsciously resting on her hips. Where was he? Had Ward changed his plans and sent Court somewhere else? She *had* to see him.

Suddenly a strong arm grabbed Kendra around the waist. A hand clamped across her mouth. She panicked, trying to scream, but only a whimper escaped through the fingers. Desperately she scrabbled at the heavy hand, but it was useless. *It's those awful men*, she thought in despair. *I just know it. They saw right through us, and they want the truth from me.*

Kendra was lifted off the ground and carried several hundred feet. She tried valiantly to kick her kidnapper, but her legs were too short. Wriggling and fighting, she was finally set down on the ground.

"What are you doing here?" Court barked as he dropped her unceremoniously.

Kendra stared up at him. Relief washed over her as she realized she was safe. Throwing her arms around his neck, she showered kisses over his frowning face.

"Kendra, stop," he said sternly, tugging her arms from around his neck.

"You scared me to death, Court. Why didn't you just tell me it was you? I thought I was being kidnapped—or worse." A small shiver ran down Kendra's spine as she thought of "worse."

"Why were you sneaking around out here?" He glared angrily down at Kendra. "Are you meeting someone?"

"As a matter of fact I am." Relieved to see Court, Kendra didn't notice his anger.

"Who?"

"Who?" Kendra repeated, frowning. What a silly question! Who would she be meeting but Court?

"That's right. Who are you meeting?" Court persisted stubbornly.

Kendra finally took a closer look at her beloved's face. His mouth was set in a stern line, the muscles in his jaw clenched, and his eyes glittered angrily.

"Court," she said, taking a step closer. "What's the matter with you?"

Court immediately turned his back and walked a few paces away. "I think you should go, Kendra."

Kendra stared, unable to believe what he was saying. "You want me to leave?"

"Yes."

"But why?" Kendra asked in astonishment. "Why are you angry with me?" Grabbing Court's arm, she tried to get him to face her.

"It doesn't matter, Kendra. I just think it would be best if you left." Shoulders slumped, he refused to turn around.

Kendra still didn't understand. "Do you have to get back to work? Do you think someone will see us together?"

Court shook his head. He'd been thinking hard about what to do after seeing Kendra with Joshua Douglas, and he'd made his decision. It wasn't going to be easy, but it had to be done. For Kendra's sake. Silently he prayed for the courage to speak his next words.

"Kendra, it's over."

"What's over?" she asked.

Court's pain made his words sharp. "We're over. You and me."

"But why?" Kendra whispered in shock. What was happening? Court loved her. He had told her time and time again. Had he changed his mind?

"I don't want to talk about it right now, Kendra. Just leave."

Bravely Kendra kept the tears at bay. She had no idea what was going on, but she wouldn't allow herself to show weakness. Her pride was the only thing that would get her through this.

"All right, Court, I'll go if that's what you want."

Shoulders straight, Kendra turned and walked away. But try as she might, she could not stifle the sob that broke from her throat. She tried to regain her control quickly. Court didn't want her. The man she had loved since arriving in South Carolina was telling her to leave him. It made no sense. She sobbed again.

"Kendra," Court moaned.

Without hesitation, Kendra turned and ran to him, flinging her arms around his neck. Agonizing sobs shook her. Clinging to him, she buried her face in his neck. It didn't matter that his powerful arms crushed her. It felt good to be held, even if it was for the last time.

After a moment, she spoke, her face still pressed to Court's shoulder.

"What did you say?" he asked.

Kendra kept her head down, repeating herself clearly. "Do you love someone else?"

When he did not answer right away Kendra's worst fears were confirmed. *He does love someone else!* Pulling free, she fled to the foot of a tree and drew her knees up tight against her chest. She rocked back and forth while the tears slid down her cheeks.

"Why do you ask me that?" Court finally asked.

"Why else would you tell me it was over between us?" Didn't Court remember the way he'd saved her life on the docks in Charleston? The kiss they'd shared there? How could he be so cold?

"I don't want to send you away," he said harshly. "But can't stand aside and watch *you* love another. You're breaking my heart."

Kendra looked at Court, wondering if he were joking. But there was no laughter in those deep green eyes—only pain.

"How can you think me such a fickle woman after the time we've spent together? Haven't I pledged myself to you, Courtland Yardley?" At his reluctant nod, Kendra continued, "Haven't I stood by your decision not to speak to my father until your indenture is done? I don't change my affections with my clothing, Mr. Yardley. When I give my heart to a man, I'm pledged to him forever."

Flinching as if Kendra had struck him, Court turned his back. "You don't have to lie to me, Kendra. I've seen you."

"Lie to you?" Kendra exclaimed, jumping up. "I have never lied to you. Ever. And what is it that you think you've seen?"

Court turned to glare at her. "I've seen the way you follow Joshua Douglas around."

"Joshua?" Kendra gasped.

"Joshua, is it?"

"But, Court, you don't understand!"

Court held up his hand to halt her words. "It no longer matters, Kendra. I've had plenty of time to think about this and I think it would be better for us both if you found another man. You need someone who is good enough for you."

"You wouldn't *mind* if I loved someone else?" Kendra asked, horrified.

Court shook his head.

In desperation Kendra forgot all about her pride. "You can't leave me," she begged, running to him. "I'll never love another man. You're the only one I want."

Court was silent.

"I don't love Joshua Douglas. Uncle Ward asked me to show him around because he's interested in horses. That's all. I'm not interested in him," she pleaded.

She wished she could tell Court all about Lizy and her suspicion that Joshua was beating his slaves. But she was afraid that Court would be furious. Anxiously, she waited for his response.

"Are you sure you don't care about him?" Court asked tentatively.

"Are you deaf, Court? I love you and only you. No other man will make me happy."

Running fingers through his red hair, Court shook his head in misery. "It won't work, Kendra. We've been kidding ourselves. Your family will want you to marry an influential husband. That certainly isn't me. I think the best thing is not to see each other. You'll find someone else to love."

Kendra turned to stone. Angry splotches colored her cheeks. She had been waiting two years for Court to be released from being indentured, and now he was telling her to find someone else two months before he was free.

"Very well." Her voice was icy. "If that's the way you want it. I hope you find happiness and love with whomever you choose."

Kendra marched away. She refused to throw herself at a man who didn't want her. Her heart breaking, she leaped into her saddle and was off like a shot.

Flying through the woods at breakneck speed, trying to outrun the pain that was clutching her heart, Kendra was oblivious to the world around her. The day had held such promise. But the joke was on her; Court didn't want her anymore. The wind snatched her tears from her eyes, stinging her flushed cheeks. The thundering of Turnip's hooves pounded in her head.

Breaking free of the trees, Kendra continued racing across the fields. She knew she should slow down, but the pain was suffocating her. Instead of heading back to Catawba she wheeled Turnip around and headed toward the road. Ahead of her was another large forest. She drove Turnip forward into the trees. They were dense and dark, nothing like the woods where Court had been working. As Kendra finally realized the danger of her headlong rush, she eased back on Turnip's reins.

Suddenly she saw a large log blocking the path. It was too late to pull Turnip to a complete stop. They would have to jump it. But before they could get off the ground, Kendra felt Turnip's hoof catch on something. The jolt almost unseated her. Stumbling slightly, Turnip tried to regain her balance. With each step her hooves slipped and skidded. Snorting and screaming, the horse valiantly tried to right herself while Kendra clung tightly to the saddle, her knuckles white. She was too frightened to kick loose and jump off. Trees and vines flew past them, and then her world was turning upside down.

Turnip fell with a final squeal, and Kendra flung her arms out hoping to break the fall. The damp ground rushed toward her.

Laurel felt hot and sticky. Her face and hands were scratched from the overgrowth she'd had to crawl into. Her hair hung in an untidy braid down her back. She was tired.

Pickle had spent the last several hours teaching her to distinguish between different animal tracks and the types of traps used to catch those animals. It was more difficult than she had realized. But Laurel wasn't about to give up and let Joshua Douglas win their wager. She would do her best and hope that it was enough. Even if she lost, it would have been fun trying to wipe the smug look Joshua always seemed to have right off his face.

When she and Pickle walked back into the camp, they found her rival propped against a tree. He was sound asleep. Angry at seeing the man so at ease in the swamp when she was so miserable, Laurel walked over and kicked his leg as hard as she could. She smiled at his grunt of pain.

"Get up, Mr. Douglas. It's time to start our wager."

Joshua tipped back his hat and watched as Laurel marched to the center of the camp and waited for him to join her. He was captivated by the glittering blue of her eyes. *She's even more stunning than I remembered,* he thought with some surprise. Getting to his feet, he joined her.

"I'm ready when you are, Miss Marston."

"Very well." Her arms crossed over her chest, Laurel began dictating the rules. "We hunt for two hours. Pickle has a timepiece and will fire a shot into the air when our time is up. Whatever we have caught at that time, we bring back to camp. Whoever brings back the most is the winner. If we both end up with the same amount, then we'll go by the size of the animal we caught."

"That sounds fair," Joshua said, tipping his head in agreement.

"We shall go in opposite directions, so as not to run into each other or frighten the other's game. We wouldn't want someone calling foul."

"I wouldn't dream of calling you a cheater, Miss Marston." Joshua's eyes glinted with amusement. This was going to be quite an amusing affair.

"Shall we begin?" Laurel turned to Pickle, who had silently watched the whole exchange. "Two hours, Pickle, then fire a shot." Without another look at her opponent, Laurel headed into the swamp.

Pickle sat back and chuckled. "I wouldn't be in your shoes for anythin' in the world, Master Douglas."

Joshua grinned back. "Oh, I have a feeling Miss Marston's bark is worse than her bite." With a wave, he left the clearing.

Pickled shook his head, chuckling again. "I wouldn't be too sure of that, Master Douglas. I wouldn't be too sure."

Minutes later, Laurel trudged through the thick weeds. Finding just the right spot to set the traps as Pickle had taught was taking longer than she'd planned. She knew the wager was ridiculous and that her chances of winning were slim. Laurel prayed she'd find an entire family of rabbits who would throw themselves into her hands. She laughed at her silly idea.

After a bit more searching, she finally found some likely spots and painstakingly set her traps before retreating to a safe distance. Quietly and patiently she waited, taking the time to recuperate from the day's activity. She could only guess at the time. Finally, she judged that the two hours were nearing their end.

Biting her lip in anticipation, Laurel returned to her traps and carefully checked them one by one. By the time she reached the last one, her disappointment was overwhelming. Only three small rabbits. Three. After all of her hard work and determination. Joshua would easily be able to top that.

Sighing in frustration, she tied her catch together and began the trek back to camp just as a shot rang out. Not too much later, she reached the clearing. Strolling over to Pickle, she tossed the rabbits down at his feet.

"Not too good," she mumbled dispiritedly.

"You did good, Missy Laurel. 'Member this be your first time." Pickle's praise did little to boost Laurel's spirits. "Let ole Pickle take care of puttin' these in the fire. You go rest."

Thankfully Laurel collapsed onto her sleeping roll. It felt good to be so exhausted. She felt like she hadn't had a rest in years. She closed her eyes and dozed while Pickle skinned her rabbits and set them on a spit over the fire.

"My, my, my. What happened to you?" Pickle's laughter pulled Laurel from her rest. Wondering what he was talking about, she opened her eyes. Her jaw dropped.

Joshua Douglas stood there, covered in mud. His hair was plastered to his head; his clothes were unrecognizable. His blue eyes shone from a black mask of earth. He was a walking mass of swamp.

Laurel jumped up in concern. "What happened? Are you all right?" She ran her eyes over his body, looking for injuries.

"Do I look all right?" Joshua answered testily.

"Well . . . you look kind of dirty." Laurel's lip began to twitch as she realized he wasn't hurt.

Joshua's lips thinned. Glaring at her, he haughtily walked to the fire and stripped off his shirt. "Isn't there any clean water in this place I can wash with?" he grumbled.

"There be a small stream not far from here that should do," Pickle volunteered.

"Fine. Can you show me where?" Pointedly ignoring Laurel, Joshua stomped out of the clearing in the direction Pickle had indicated. Silently shaking with laughter, the old man followed.

Laurel stood alone, bemused. She was still reacting to the sight of Joshua Taylor with his shirt off. He was the most beautiful man she had ever seen in her life. The muscles in his arms and back. . . . Lost in her reverie, she barely caught the amused glance Pickle gave her as he returned.

Disgusted with herself, Laurel crouched next to the fire. Carefully she lifted one of the small rabbits that she had caught and, sliding it onto a large piece of clean bark, handed it to Pickle.

"Looks mighty good, Missy Laurel. I'll make a good woodsman out of you yet."

"You're the best teacher anyone could ask for." In spite of herself, Laurel smiled with pleasure. She picked up her own rabbit.

Pickle scanned the trees. "Wonder what's takin' that young man of yours so long."

"He's not my man!" sputtered Laurel, dropping her meat onto the ground in agitation. A pink flush spread across her cheeks as Pickle began to laugh.

"Now, Missy Laurel, you can't lie to ole Pickle. I know what my eyes tells me, and they be tellin' me you like that young man."

Lifting her chin a fraction, Laurel refused to look at him. "I can assure you, Pickle, that Joshua Douglas means nothing to me. Besides, I'll be marrying my Jason soon, and he's the only one for me."

"Mmm-hmmm."

Scornfully Laurel retrieved her fallen rabbit, cleaned it off, and bit into it ravenously. *Who could blame a person for enjoying the sight of Joshua without his shirt?* she thought. *That's all it is—an appreciation of his handsomeness. Besides, Jason Portland will be here soon, and he is who I want to marry.*

Chewing a bite of meat, Laurel unwillingly thought about what Marissa had said to her last week. Joshua had seemed happy enough to kiss Marissa. Would he be as accommodating to Laurel herself? If she was to have experience, as Marissa had said men expected, then perhaps Joshua could provide that experience. She wanted to be the best of wives to Jason. But how could she get Joshua to kiss her? Marissa had asked him to, but Laurel didn't think she could be so forward. It wouldn't be proper. And if anyone ever found out, she'd be humiliated.

Lost in thought, Laurel was startled to realize that a pair of wet breeches were standing in front of her. She looked up into Joshua's carefully blank expression.

"You have won the wager, Miss Marston. I believe your request was to have a compliment from me." Stiffly, Joshua bowed. "You are truly an amazing woman. I have never met before, and doubt I ever will meet again, a woman who is so full of surprises. I have misjudged you and I apologize."

"Thank you, Mr. Douglas," she murmured. "Would you like some rabbit?"

"Yes, thank you." Surprise flickered briefly in his eyes. He had steeled himself for a gloating response. But without a word, Laurel stood and went to the fire to retrieve the third rabbit she'd caught. He took it warily and seated himself beside her. Silence reigned for a moment as all three of them ate.

"What happened?" Laurel finally asked.

Joshua snorted as he took a bite of the succulent rabbit. He didn't want to tell the story to anyone, especially Laurel Marston. He had a feeling she'd find it quite amusing.

"You're not going to tell us?" she asked in amazement when he didn't speak.

"No, I am not."

Laurel was annoyed at his tone. "Fine."

"Fine."

Pickle stood and excused himself. "I gonna fetch firewood for the night."

"I'll help," Laurel volunteered, jumping up quickly.

"Nah. You keep that fella company."

Laurel watched Pickle leave. With the older man gone, she realized that now was a perfect opportunity to bring up the subject of kissing. How did one do such a thing? She'd never been kissed in her life. What would it feel like? More importantly, how did one go about it?

Laurel blushed at the turn her thoughts were taking. She was nervous. She was alone in the swamp with a man. Her father would never approve of this. If anyone ever found out, her reputation would be in shreds. She wondered if Marissa would be proud of her behavior. Or jealous?

"Why are you so nervous, Miss Laurel?" Joshua questioned.

Laurel jumped at the sound of his voice. "Nervous? I'm not nervous."

"Are you sure I don't make you nervous, Miss Laurel?" Joshua asked softly, moving to stand in front of her. Unable to answer, Laurel slowly shook her head. Her breath caught in her throat, and the acceleration of her heart made her dizzy. *Do something*, she told herself. All she could think of was kissing him.

"I'm glad. Because right at this moment I want to kiss you." Joshua looked down at Laurel. She froze in shock, her eyes huge and blue. *Is this really happening?* she thought wildly. Cupping her face in his hands, he lowered his head until their lips were only a breath apart.

"You're the most desirable woman I've ever met," he whispered before claiming her lips with his own.

A tingling sensation began at Laurel's toes and consumed her entire body. Joshua's arms wrapped firmly around her, nearly crushing her. She tried to press herself closer. She felt on fire. *So this is what it feels like,* she thought incoherently. Never had she dreamed a kiss could be so good. It was as if Joshua Douglas were branding her as his own.

She had to bite back the cry that almost burst from her as Joshua lifted his head. A storm raged in the depths of his eyes and, startled by its intensity, she pulled from his hold.

"Well, well, well," Joshua commented stiffly as Laurel took a step back. "I must say, Miss Laurel Marston, you are definitely not the proper young lady I thought."

Laurel's head jerked back as if she'd been struck, and she reacted without thought. Raising her hand, she slapped Joshua across the cheek as hard as she could, the sound shattering the still night.

"And you, sir, are no gentleman."

Cammie ran into Taylor's room, agitated. "Miss Taylor, them three men are back askin' to see you. I didn't know what to do."

"It's all right, Cammie. Calm down. Has Ward come in yet?"

"Yes. He's down in the barn."

"Very well. Would you tell the gentlemen to wait on the porch while I go have a talk with Ward?" Taylor went out at the back of the house, not wanting to run into the men. Finding Ward in the barn, she pulled him aside.

"We have company," she whispered.

"Who? And why are you whispering?"

"Three men are looking for a runaway slave girl and they want to search the plantation. I told them they would have to wait for you to return before they could look around." Taylor tugged nervously on her lower lip. She hated getting Ward involved.

"I take it we have a guest here?" At Taylor's nod, Ward winced. "All right. I'll take care of the men. Where's Kendra?"

"I don't know. She went out riding right after they left and I haven't seen her since." Taylor had been busy with Brooke for most of the day. Now that she had time to think about Kendra, she suddenly realized that a whole day had passed since she'd seen her niece. As impetuous as Kendra was, it wasn't like her to be absent for so long.

"When was that?"

A worried frown creased her forehead. "This morning."

Ward went to Turnip's stall and saw that it was empty. "Joseph," he bellowed. A young boy scurried from the tack room. "Has Miss Kendra come back from her ride?"

"No, sir."

"Have you seen her at all since she left?"

"No, sir."

Taylor and Ward looked at each other. Both of them knew the seriousness of a young girl lost in the wilderness that surrounded their home. Taylor gripped Ward's arm. "I'm worried, Ward. She's been gone a long time. We need to look for her right away."

"I know. You stay here and ask if anyone knows which direction she rode. I'll go talk to Yates."

Ward ran up to the house, completely ignoring the three men who stood by the porch steps. Slamming into the hall, he burst into the office, startling his brother. Yates was quick to sense Ward's urgency.

"What's wrong?" Yates immediately stood.

"It's Kendra. She hasn't come back from her ride. She's been gone since morning. We need to make a search for her before the sun goes down."

Yates didn't waste any time. "Let's go."

As the two men left the house, they ran into Pete and his men. By now, Ward had forgotten what Taylor had told him regarding the trackers. Pete boldly stepped forward. "Is one of you Marston?"

Thinking that they might have news of Kendra, Yates and Ward instantly halted. "Yes," said Ward. "We're Ward and Yates Marston. What do you want?"

"We're here to search your plantation for a runaway slave. We was told to come back and you'd let us look 'round."

Yates looked at the dirty man with contempt. "I couldn't care less about your runaway slave." Pete started to protest, but Yates overrode him. "Listen, man. My daughter is missing and we have to find her before it gets dark. Now, unless you're going to make yourself useful and help us look for her, I suggest you get out of my way."

Seeing the dangerous look in Yates's eyes, Pete hesitated. A crafty look came over his face. "If we help you look, will you let us search your place for the runaway?"

Angered beyond his limit, Yates would have made a lunge for the man if Ward hadn't stepped between them. "Very well," Ward replied. "You help us search until we find her. Afterward, you may freely search our buildings. Okay?"

Pete nodded warily, staying clear of Yates. "Come on, boys.

Within minutes, Yates and Ward had called in every available man and organized a search. They would scour the woods and the surrounding fields. Someone was sent to Jacob Ferguson's place for his dogs; he had the best trackers around. Armed with lanterns, they scattered across Catawba.

Court came into the yard just as the search began. Curious at the commotion, he found Ward and Yates. "What's happening?"

"We're searching for Kendra." Yates's voice was stiff with worry.

"What?"

"She's been missing since this morning. No one has seen her since she left. Grab a lantern and come on."

Court swallowed a groan. He actually felt physically ill with worry. His Kendra was missing. What could have happened to her? Trying desperately to hide his feelings, he nodded. "What section do want me to search?"

Court was soon out with the rest of the men. He searched his designated area thoroughly. How he wished he could take back the words he had spoken earlier. If something terrible had happened to her, he would never forgive himself. He bowed his head.

"Father God, You know where Kendra is. Please protect her. Keep her safe from any harm. And help us to find her quickly. Amen."

Laurel stared in disbelief at what she'd just done. She was not in the habit of lashing out in anger. But Joshua Douglas had a way of stirring her emotions beyond their usual limits. He seemed to take pleasure in making her lose her calm demeanor. And he had truly done it this time.

She watched Joshua rub the vivid red hand print on his cheek. She would have apologized, but his glaring look flustered her.

"Tell me something, Miss Marston," Joshua said stonily. "Do all your young men get treated in such a fashion?" When Laurel made no move to answer, he continued. "Or perhaps you're the type that doesn't care for physical contact. Dangle your beauty in front of their noses, but if they touch you, you pull away."

Laurel was astonished. Opening and closing her mouth several times, she found no words to express herself. How could he say such horrible things about her? He was calling her a tease.

"You may be even worse than that," Joshua continued. "Could it be that you're so frigid you can't respond to a man's touch? Does it shock your sensibilities to have a real man hold you and stir your desire?" A mirthless chuckle grated Laurel's nerves. "I see you're surprised by my observations, Miss Marston. Don't worry, I'm not one to kiss and tell.

"It won't be too difficult for you to find a man willing to marry an icicle. Some men prefer to keep their own room and not share their wife's after the marriage. With your family's money, you should be able to persuade someone on that one stipulation." Joshua's lip curled in disgust as he gathered up his bed roll, shoved it in his pack, and walked away.

"How dare you say such horrible things to me!" Laurel cried.

"You don't care for the truth, Miss Marston?" Joshua snarled.

"That's not the truth," she countered. She was anything but frigid. In fact, Laurel had never felt so alive. She could still feel the pressure of his kiss on her mouth. Curling her fingers into the sides of her riding habit, she refused to allow her traitorous hand to touch her lips.

Whispered conversations with girlfriends in England were all Laurel knew of what happened between a man and a woman. They hadn't prepared her for what Joshua made her feel. She knew it wasn't proper to respond as she had, but she couldn't help it. When Joshua had said she was no proper lady, Laurel had responded impulsively. Being a lady was important in finding a suitable husband, and she prided herself on it. No man wanted a wanton woman . . . did he?

"Where are you going?" Laurel demanded.

"As far away from you as I can get."

His footsteps faded away as she sank to the ground, shivering. What had she done? Lost in her own misery, she didn't hear Pickle return to camp.

"You all right, Missy Laurel?" asked Pickle worriedly.

Laurel nodded.

"That young man gone?"

She nodded again.

"You ever gonna talk to ole Pickle again?"

Laurel gazed up at the old man who had become her friend. Tears slid down her cheeks. She knew Pickle had heard everything. Nothing ever got by him.

"I'll be fine, Pickle. Don't worry." Laurel tried to speak with confidence, but her voice quivered.

Pickle patted her arm. "That young man is hurtin' real bad. He'll get over it and come arunnin'. You'll see."

"No," Laurel whispered. "I don't want him to come. I don't ever want to see him again." She knew the words were a lie, but she forced herself to continue. "Jason Portland is the man I want to marry. He's a perfect gentleman, and that's who I want to spend the rest of my life with."

"A perfect gentleman ain't always the perfect person," Pickle said wisely.

It was completely dark when everyone regrouped. No one had seen even a trace of Kendra. Not even Jacob Ferguson's dogs could find her. Court was beside himself with worry. He stood with Yates, Ward, and Ferguson, discussing the best way to proceed.

"The men have searched all the fields and a short distance into the woods." Yates paced restlessly.

"Any idea where she would have gone?" Ward asked.

"I don't know. My daughters never tell me their plans. And you know Kendra. She disappears for hours on end." He shook his head. "Well, she won't after this."

"What about workers?" asked Jacob. "We haven't asked them. Someone must have seen her."

Court knew he had to say something. "I saw Miss Kendra earlier."

Yates wheeled on him. "Why didn't you say anything sooner, man?" he shouted.

"Because it was before noon and there's no telling where she went." Court couldn't say anymore. How could he tell Yates that he and Kendra had broken off their plans to marry?

"Did she say anything about where she was going?" questioned Ward.

"No, sir."

"Did she seem all right?" Ward persisted.

"Well, sir, she was upset. But she didn't say where she was going. As a matter of fact, I thought she was heading home."

"Why?"

"Because she turned back toward Catawba." Court was silent, hoping they wouldn't question him further.

After a lengthy discussion, the brothers decided to check farther down the road. The dogs were loaded into a wagon along with Yates, Ward, Court, and Jacob Ferguson. Silently, Court drove them down the lane. He willed Kendra to be there.

"This is as good a spot as any," Yates called after a while. His voice was harsh over the creaking of the wagon and the barking dogs.

Court steered the wagon toward the edge of the trees. Jumping down, he helped the men gather the dogs and started toward the woods.

"You stay here, Court," Ward ordered.

"But you need my help," Court insisted.

"No, stay here with the team. We don't want anything to happen to them. We'll fire one shot into the air if we find her." Ward slapped Court on the shoulder. "We'll find her—we've got to."

Watching the men and dogs moving slowly forward into the trees, Court paced around the wagon. The barking was soon a hollow echo.

Kendra's eyes slowly fluttered open. Seeing nothing but darkness, she tried to get up. Pain shot through her skull, exploding behind her eyes. Groaning, she lifted a muddy hand to her head. When she felt well enough to open her eyes again, she surveyed the area. In the dark, all she could see were trees surrounding the small clearing in which she lay. The night sky was filled with stars, and there was a slight chill in the air. She could hear nothing.

Feeling a heavy weight on her leg, Kendra looked down. Turnip lay there unmoving, her neck unnaturally twisted. Tears filled Kendra's eyes as she realized her horse was dead. Miserably, she laid her head back, trying to remember what had happened.

She remembered turning Turnip into the forest. There was a log . . . Turnip tripping . . . falling . . . her shoulder slamming into something. . . . Kendra began to weep. Her day had gone from bad to worse. It had started with those horrible men questioning her about Lizy. It had worsened with Court telling her that he no longer wanted to marry her. Now her beloved Turnip was gone, and she was alone here in the night.

Kendra continued crying until shivers racked her slim body as the chill seeped into her bones. The more she shivered, the more the fog of pain eased away. Finally, beginning to realize the severity of her situation, she tried to consider her options.

First was freeing herself. Her leg was pinned underneath Turnip's weight, but try as she might, she could not shift the mare. She bit her lip to keep from crying out as her wrenched muscles protested the abuse. The pain in her head settled to a dull throb.

"I have to get out of here," she whispered. But how? *Father God*, she prayed silently, *show me the best way to get out of here. Help me return to Catawba safely.*

Looking down, Kendra saw that the soft ground under her would be easy to dig. She began gouging out the earth with her hands, heedless of the damage to her fingers and nails. It was going to work, she realized, but it wasn't going fast enough. Reaching for a large stick, she began to scrape away the dirt around her leg.

After what seemed like an eternity, she was able to wiggle free. Her leg was bruised and her whole body ached, but thanks to the damp soil, nothing seemed to be broken.

The exertion had increased the pounding in her head, however. Trying not to sob, she closed her eyes briefly, hoping the pain would ease, then slowly got to her feet. It wouldn't help if she stood too quickly and fainted. She had to stay alert and think clearly.

Next, she pressed her lips into a determined line and took a slow, tentative step. Yes, she would be able to walk. But to where? She had no idea in which direction she should go. As she limped out of the clearing, she furrowed her brow, listening closely to the night sounds. She thought she could hear dogs barking. Dogs? What were dogs doing in the forest? Why were they making so much noise? The questions made her head hammer. *No more thinking,* she told herself and continued her slow steps.

When she saw that she had made it to the road, Kendra paused to lean against a large tree. Taking deep, steadying breaths, she tried to get her bearings. She couldn't remember how far she had ridden, and she hoped Catawba wasn't much farther. It had seemed to take hours just getting this far. She thought that if she cut across the corner of the forest, she could save some time. That's what she'd do, she decided.

"I just want to go home," she muttered as she wearily pushed away from the tree and continued moving forward. "I just want to go home."

Court stood rigidly at the edge of the trees. He could hear the dogs, but wasn't sure what, if anything, their barking meant. Why hadn't they found her yet?

The sliver of moon cast little light. The barking dogs seemed to have moved further away. Following the sound, Court walked along the tree edge. His attention was focused on the forest, listening intently for the shot that would indicate Kendra had been found. As he continued down the line of trees, oblivious to his steps, he tripped and sprawled face down in the deep weeds. Muttering, he climbed to his feet. This was ridiculous—no one should have to endure such painful waiting.

Suddenly, he froze. He had heard something—a small groan. Not moving a muscle, he listened carefully. Was it just an animal noise?

When he heard the sound again, Court began running toward it. Could it be Kendra? *Dear God, please let it be her,* he prayed fervently. As the noises grew louder, his search grew more frantic. Where was she? He could hear her, but he couldn't see her.

"Kendra," Court called, hoping she would be able to answer him. "Kendra, it's Court. Where are you? I can't find you," he called desperately.

"Court," Kendra moaned.

She sounded so close. Court plowed through the weeds until he almost fell over Kendra's body propped against a tree. Dropping on his knees, he buried his face in her neck. He couldn't stop the tears. She was alive. That was all that mattered. His Kendra was alive.

"Where are you hurt?" he asked a moment later.

"Everywhere," she whispered.

"Will it hurt you too much if I lift you? The wagon isn't far. I'll take you back to Catawba." With gentle hands, Court lifted Kendra and carried her back to the wagon. Carefully, he placed her in the back. When he was sure she was comfortable, he raised his long gun and fired a shot into the air.

Court knew he had to get Kendra home immediately, but it would take the other men a while to get back to the wagon. Climbing into the wagon, he snapped the horses into motion and turned them toward Catawba.

Kendra moaned. The small movement of her head brought another spasm of pain. Gentle hands lifted her head and held a glass to her parched lips.

"How is she?" asked Maida, slipping into the darkened room.

"She just woke for a moment. I gave her a drink, but I'm worried about her fever." Taylor pushed wisps of Kendra's hair back from her face, a concerned frown clouding her expression.

"Do you think she'll be all right?"

"I pray that she will be. Have Yates and Ward returned yet?" Taylor asked.

"Not yet. They should be home soon, though. As soon as Court dropped Kendra off he went back for them." Maida stood at the foot of the bed looking down at Kendra. "If it hadn't been for Court, who knows when we might have found her."

Taylor and Maida had been sitting in the front room, waiting nervously for news. Without warning, the front door had burst open with Court carrying Kendra in his arms. When the women reached the hall, they had been shocked. Kendra was covered in mud. Her dress was torn and her body bruised and scratched from her ordeal. Taylor had run her hands over Kendra, but found no broken bones, just a severe cut on her head.

"She's all right, Taylor," Court had said impatiently. "Where should I put her?"

"We'll take her to her room," Taylor ordered, then turned to Maida. "Have Cammie bring plenty of hot water. We'll need to clean her up before we can tend to her wounds."

Taylor led Court up the stairs and into Kendra's bedroom. Gently, he placed her on the pillow, stared at her for a moment, then quietly left. Taylor pulled off Kendra's muddy boots and riding clothes. A moment later Cammie and Maida came bustling in carrying buckets of steaming hot water.

"I already had water goin', Miss Taylor. I know we was gonna need it," Cammie said. "The tub is on the way up."

"Thank you, Cammie."

Together the women cleaned the dried mud from Kendra's body. It was so thick in places they could scrape it off with their fingernails. The clamminess of Kendra's skin frightened Taylor. They would have to get her warm before putting her to bed.

"Cammie, hurry with the tub."

"What's wrong, Taylor?" Maida asked.

"We have to get her warm. She was outside so long her skin got chilled. Would you get the blanket from the bed, Maida?"

Maida pulled the blanket off the bed and wrapped it around Kendra, tucking it close around her. "Is there anything else I can do?"

"Pray," said Taylor.

Moments later, a large tub was brought into the room. Servants dumped steaming buckets of water into it. Lifting Kendra's still unconscious body, Maida and Taylor set her in the hot water.

Kendra still hadn't opened her eyes or made any sound when they lifted her from the tub minutes later. *If only she would say something,* Taylor thought. As she wrapped Kendra in a soft muslin dressing gown, she checked the wound on her head. It was turning a dark shade of purple. The gash was clean, but deeper than Taylor had first thought. Smoothing ointment over it, she carefully bandaged the cut.

Taylor and Maida knelt beside the bed. Bowing their heads the two women prayed over their girl.

Not long after, Yates burst into the bedroom with Ward close on his heels. The sight of Maida and Taylor by the bed brought them to an abrupt halt.

"Kendra!"

"She's unconscious, Yates," said Taylor. Standing, she crossed the room. "She's had a wound to the head, but I think she'll be all right." Taylor laid a hand on his shoulder.

"How do you know?" Yates asked worriedly.

"We've done everything we can. Now we pray and wait. She's strong. She should be fine."

Yates took halting steps toward the bed and knelt beside Maida. Together they clasped hands and prayed for their daughter.

Ward wrapped a comforting arm around Taylor. "You did a fine job, honey. We'll have to trust in God now." Taylor leaned against Ward, letting his strength revive her aching muscles.

They were still like that when Cammie walked into the room. "You all go to bed now. I watch over Miss Kendra."

"No, I'll stay with her, Cammie," said Maida.

"Now, Miss Maida, there be no arguin' with me. You gotta take care of your child. I take fine care of Miss Kendra." Cammie refused to take any argument and after a last look, the family filed out of the room.

Pulling a chair over to the bed, Cammie sat and took Kendra's hand. "Now you listen here, Miss Kendra. You gonna get all better and there better be no arguin' with Cammie. I know what I talkin' 'bout. Your family be real worried 'bout you and that not good."

Family's the worst to watch over the sick, she mused. *They worry too hard for the sick one to get better*. Sighing, she made herself comfortable in her chair. It was going to be a long night.

Cammie remained on her vigil throughout the night. Every-half hour she'd try to spoon water down Kendra's throat, but it wasn't until the sun peeked over the horizon that Kendra finally lifted her lids. She slowly moved her head.

Cammie put her hand on Kendra's forehead. "So our little lost girl is back from the dead." Kendra opened her mouth to speak, but no sound would come out. Cammie lifted her head and helped her take a drink of water.

"Now don't you go talkin' yet. You need plenty of rest. Are you hungry?" asked Cammie.

Kendra nodded, wincing at the pain in her head.

"Don't you worry none 'bout that headache. It'll go away with time. I'll go downstairs to get you some food, if'n you promise not to move." Cammie paused. "Your family is gonna be real glad to see you awake."

Down in the kitchen, Cammie heaped a plateful of food onto a tray along with juice. Carefully she carried it back up to Kendra's room. "Here we are, Miss Kendra. I brought you scrambled eggs and fresh juice. That should be easy 'nough for you to swallow."

Before she placed the tray across the bed, Cammie glanced at the patient. Kendra was sound asleep. Checking her forehead for any signs of fever, Cammie smiled. The worst was over.

Laurel heaved the gown over her head. She adjusted it carefully to make sure it hid the swamp outfit underneath.

"What you gonna do if'n your pa finds out about that outfit you got on under that dress?" Pickle asked.

Forcing a laugh, Laurel considered the possible consequences. "Everyone all the way to Charleston would probably hear his reaction if he found out. You know how vocal my father is when he's angry."

"What about the fancy fella you wanna marry?"

"Jason? What about him?" asked Laurel, puzzled.

"You gonna show him what you wearin' out here?"

Laurel had never thought about what Jason would think of her excursions. The only person she'd ever had to keep anything from was her father. What would she do if Jason refused to let her go into the swamp? Laurel shrugged. She was too tired; she would worry about the future later.

"Makes no sense to me why them men can't be proud of the things you learned since coming here. You a part of America now. That's good."

Laurel thought about that. She *was* a part of this rugged country. Coming to the new land had been a nightmare, but with Pickle's help Laurel was learning to take care of herself. It felt good to know that she could rely on her own abilities to get out of trouble. She stood a little straighter and thrust her chin up, defying anyone to make her be less than she was.

In England she'd been taught that she was only good for marriage and having children. But at Catawba, Laurel knew she was worth more than that. She could hunt, cook, and take care of the sick. Humming softly, she followed Pickle out of the clearing. They should be back by late afternoon. As much as she enjoyed these trips, it would be good to have a nice hot bath and sleep in her own bed tonight.

Several hours later, they reached the well in front of the Catawba cabins. Weary, hungry, and thirsty, Laurel was thankful to be home. She left Pickle at his small cabin and headed for the big house.

The stillness of the front hall surprised her, but too weary to investigate, she headed for her bedroom, desire for a bath quickening her steps. She would have Cammie order the tub for her. She envisioned relaxing while the warm water soaked the dirt off of her tired body.

As she reached the door to her bedroom, she glanced across the hall to Kendra's and stopped in surprise. The entire family stood around Kendra's bed, talking in low tones.

"What's going on?" she asked, crossing over.

"Laurel." Jumping up, Maida came around and hugged the grimy girl.

"What's going on?" Laurel repeated, looking from one family member to another. Then she noticed Kendra propped up against the pillows, bandaged and pale.

"Everything is fine now. Kendra had an accident with Turnip yesterday, but she's recovering." Maida patted Laurel's hand, drawing her over to the bed.

"What did you do this time, Kendra?" Laurel asked gently. She was frightened at how weak and fragile her younger sister looked as she lay in the bed. Laurel was used to Kendra being healthy and full of life. This girl was listless and wan.

"I fell from Turnip and landed on my head. It happened that there was a rock in my way." Kendra smiled wearily.

Taylor placed a comforting hand on Kendra's head. "We were afraid we'd lose our little girl."

Laurel couldn't believe that she hadn't been there during the crisis. She had almost lost her sister. She and Kendra had never been terribly close, but Kendra was the only sister she had. She couldn't imagine life without her. Standing there, Laurel realized how much she actually loved her impetuous younger sister. Swallowing the lump in her throat, she tried to ease the tension.

"Well, since Kendra is doing fine I'm going to have Cammie draw a bath," she said lightly. "I'm so dirty, I don't dare hug my sister." She left the room amid the laughter that followed her remark.

Once she was in the hallway, though, tears began to roll down Laurel's cheeks. A riot of emotions had been tumbling through her since Joshua had kissed her last night. To return home and find her sister ill had pushed them to the surface. She felt like her whole life was turning upside down.

Pulling herself together, she went downstairs to the kitchen, but Cammie wasn't there, so she asked a servant to have a tub of water prepared. She didn't feel ready to face the crowd upstairs. After a moment's hesitation, she retreated to Brooke's room. Cammie sat there in a chair near the sleeping child, sewing on a dress.

"Miss Laurel, you back from the swamp already?"

"Yes," Laurel answered wearily. Cammie eyed her sharply.

"Your sister is doin' just fine, Miss Laurel."

"Would you mind bringing me a fresh dress, Cammie? I don't want to have to go back to my room until I'm cleaned up."

"'Course I will, Miss Laurel. Any dress you be wantin' in particular?"

"You choose one for me, Cammie. I'm too tired to even decide."

After Cammie left, Laurel peered down at the little girl lying in bed. Light brown hair was all that could be seen of Brooke's head as she snuggled under the covers. She was a beautiful child. Smiling fondly, Laurel wondered what it would be like to hold her own daughter and rock her to sleep.

Desire for the fulfillment of marriage clutched at her heart. She wished for the strong arms of a husband to hold and comfort her. *Arms like Joshua Douglas's,* she thought. Impatiently, she shook her head. She refused to think about that hideous man. His vicious words still stung.

Cammie came in carrying Laurel's dress, followed by servants carrying the big brass tub and buckets of steaming water.

"You want some help, Miss Laurel?" asked Cammie.

"No. I think I want to be alone. Thank you, Cammie."

"You relax, Miss Laurel, and take your time. If you need anything, let me know." Cammie left the room, closing the door firmly behind her.

Laurel stripped off her filthy clothes, wrapping up her swamp outfit so she could wash it later, and climbed into the tub with a sigh of delight. First, she scrubbed her body and hair clean. Then she lay back, letting her muscles relax as she reclined. Closing her eyes, she let perspiration dot her upper lip as the steam heated her face. She felt absolutely wonderful.

A loud noise outside Brooke's window startled her, shattering her solitude. The sound of running feet drifted through the open window. Frowning at the intrusion, she wrapped a toweling cloth around her body and went to the window, pushing the drapes aside. She could hear several people calling to each other. *What's going on?* she wondered.

Laurel couldn't see anything from where she stood. Crouching lower, she opened the French doors and peeked out. As long as no one looked over she would be all right. Hugging the toweling cloth close, she bent around the doorframe and looked across the veranda.

In front of the house stood an old carriage drawn by a tired team of horses. The two people in the carriage immediately caught Laurel's attention. A parasol was open, hiding her view of the woman, but she could see a man with blonde hair ordering people around. When he turned, Laurel was able to see his face.

His fair hair was pulled back and tied with a beautiful black ribbon. The contrast of light and dark was remarkable. A straight, aristocratic nose topped the handsome mustache that precisely outlined his upper lip. Soft, pale skin made his face almost pretty.

Handsome, thought Laurel. But who was he? Someone to see Uncle Ward about horses? He seemed familiar in a dreamy sort of way. She slipped back into the bedroom and climbed into the tub, relaxing again. Closing her eyes, she envisioned the man's face. She could almost remember. . . .

"Oh no!" With a gasp, Laurel bolted straight up, eyes round in dismay. It couldn't be. Not yet! Leaping from the tub, ignoring the water dripping across the wood floor, she began throwing on her clothes as quickly as her wet body allowed.

Jason Portland had arrived at Catawba.

Maida stepped out onto the large porch and watched the scene below. Slaves were being ordered about by a man who looked like a golden-haired angel. His back was to her, but she could see that his slight frame was clothed in the finest breeches and waistcoat. He turned, and Maida's eyes widened in appreciation. His features were straight and chiseled, his skin unblemished, even creamy. Having been at Catawba for two years, Maida had almost forgotten what an English gentleman looked like.

The young man reached back into the carriage and offered his hand to a female mirror-image of himself. A petite blonde woman stepped daintily from the carriage. Seeing the weariness on the woman's face, Maida quickly went down to greet them.

"Welcome to Catawba. You must be Jason and Clair Portland. We've been expecting you."

Bowing slightly, Jason tipped his hat. "Yes, my dear lady, I am Jason and this is my sister, Clair. We are Laurel Marston's guests. And you are?"

"I beg your pardon." Dipping into a slight curtsy, Maida quickly introduced herself. "I am Maida Marston, Yates Marston's wife."

"How do you do," greeted Clair. "Laurel has mentioned you in her letters often."

Maida smiled, instantly liking the young lady. "Would you like to come inside?" she offered. "The servants will see to your baggage. You must be tired from such a long journey."

"Thank you, that would be most kind." Taking his sister's arm, Jason followed behind Maida.

"Would you like some refreshment?" Maida asked when they were seated in the parlor. "Your rooms are being prepared and should be ready shortly. Your note said you would be delayed a few days. I'm afraid we weren't quite ready for you."

"Yes, well, the accommodations we'd intended using weren't appropriate for my sister. After dispatching the messenger, we decided to come straight here instead."

"I hope it isn't an inconvenience?" Clair Portland asked worriedly.

"Of course not. I'm just sorry the rooms aren't prepared for you yet. But they will be soon enough, and then you can rest."

"That sounds delightful." Clair sat back against the upholstered chair, briefly closing her eyes.

"I must apologize for my sister, Mrs. Marston. The trip wasn't very easy for her. She hasn't quite recuperated." Jason smiled at Maida.

Maida returned his smile. "I quite understand. Please don't apologize."

Cammie would be busy with the house servants, preparing guest rooms, so Maida went to the kitchen for refreshments. She returned with a laden tray. Cammie entered as the Portlands were sipping their tea.

"Are the rooms finished, Cammie?" Maida asked.

"Yes, Miss Maida."

"Fine. Thank you, Cammie."

"Oh, thank you so much." Clair Portland awkwardly stood up, swaying slightly. Placing a dainty hand to her forehead, she reached out with the other to steady herself. Jason gallantly scooped her into his arms.

"Where can I put my sister?"

Blushing at the gesture of concern, Maida hurried upstairs to the room where Clair would be staying, where Jason laid his sister gently on the bed and poured a small glass of water from the bedside pitcher. He held it to Clair's lips.

"Rest, my dear. You'll feel better in no time at all."

Before they closed the door, Clair's even breathing indicated that she'd already fallen asleep.

"I'll see that someone comes to help her undress later," offered Maida.

"You are kind, Mrs. Marston. Thank you."

"You'll have this room." She indicated a door across the hall. "I hope you will be comfortable. Will you be joining the family for dinner?"

"No, I believe I should rest this evening. I'm quite exhausted myself. Would that be convenient?" he asked.

"Of course. We want you to feel at home here. Get your rest, and we'll see you tomorrow. And please do not hesitate to call if you require anything." Taking her leave, Maida went over to Laurel's room.

The sight that greeted her was surprising. Gowns had been tossed around, slippers were scattered here and there. The girls only had a few dresses between them, but from the look of the room, they had multiplied.

"What is going on in here?" she exclaimed.

"Oh, Maida," exclaimed Laurel in relief. "I thought it might be Clair." Hurrying across the room, she pulled Maida over to a chair. "Are they settled into their rooms? Do you think they'll be comfortable here? Will they be coming to dinner this evening? What do they look like?" Laurel's words tripped over each other, making Maida laugh.

"Slow down, Laurel. I'll tell you everything if you give me a chance."

As she perched on the edge of her seat, Laurel's blue eyes sparkled. "I'm listening."

Maida described Jason and Clair and even their clothes and baggage in great detail. Laurel hung on every word.

"Are they nice, Maida?"

"They seem to be. We only spoke a few words, but they were quite polite."

"I knew they would be. Why would they have changed in two years? Clair is a wonderful friend. She and I could always spend hours talking about fashion and marriage." Giggling happily, Laurel twirled around the room. She couldn't wait to spend time with her friend . . . and Jason. Thoughts of Joshua Douglas fled far away.

"It's time for Lizy to go," Taylor said to Court the next afternoon. She had been so worried about Kendra yesterday, she'd completely forgotten about the trackers wanting to search the plantation. Ward had come to her this morning to inform her that the men had returned at the crack of dawn. They had searched, found nothing, and left. They hadn't seemed very happy, Ward had said.

Taylor had been very relieved. She knew Kendra would want to know all the details, so they'd spent a few whispered moments alone discussing what to do. Pete and his men had come close to learning the truth and Taylor didn't want to jeopardize Lizy's safety any longer. They had decided to see the girl safely to the North. Even though it meant not knowing if she belonged to Joshua Douglas.

Now Taylor leaned over the railing by the corral. Brooke was having her daily riding lesson from Pickle. The little girl's laughter and shouts echoed off of the outbuildings.

"I agree," said Court.

"I'll have the papers ready for you tomorrow afternoon, and then she can leave in the evening." Taylor waved at Brooke as the little girl rode by.

"All right. Where do you want to meet?"

"We'll do the same as today. I'll make sure that Ward assigns you to work around here and then ask you to come help me. It's the only chance we'll have. With guests in the house there won't be a quiet moment."

A chuckle escaped from Court. "Those two certainly have caused an uproar with the servants. I don't think I've ever heard such complaining. There's no end to it up at the house."

Taylor groaned in agreement. Jason Portland was actually the one causing the most problems. His sister, Clair, was happy just spending time with Laurel or resting in her room. But Jason liked to command. The servants had been ordered to fetch everything from a dash of salt to a change of clothing, and they weren't happy about it.

Cammie's grumbling was the worst. She refused to work near Jason Portland. If he sat in the parlor, she would go upstairs. If he was in his room, she would find something in the barns that needed her attention. Taylor had already received an earful of complaints from her.

"I'm at a loss about what to do. Our whole family doesn't keep the servants as busy as this one man does." Taylor shook her head despairingly.

The sound of laughter, drifting across the yard behind them, made both of them turn. They glanced at each other.

"I do believe I have something to take care of right away." With a chuckle, Court marched off before the source of laughter could reach them.

Rolling her eyes skyward, Taylor turned back to the merry trio now approaching. Three blonde heads tipped together in conversation as Jason Portland escorted his sister and Laurel toward her.

"Aunt Taylor."

"Good afternoon, everyone. Are you showing your guests around Catawba, Laurel?"

"Yes. They wanted to see some of the famous horses that Uncle Ward is raising." Laurel's eyes glowed as she looked at Jason.

Taylor looked at the impeccably attired young man. He certainly was a dandy. She knew that those delicate hands had not put in a hard day's work his whole life. The Portlands were quite well known in England. Even Taylor had heard of them.

"Well, enjoy yourselves. I'll see you this evening at dinner." Taylor called to Brooke and waited for her daughter to run across the corral to her side.

"Mrs. Marston," Clair said softly, "if you are heading back to the house, would you mind my accompanying you? I'm suddenly quite weary and in need of a nap."

"Certainly," said Taylor. She had liked Clair from the start. Maybe it was because the girl seemed so frail.

Brooke tugged at Taylor's arm. "Come on, Mommy. Cammie promised me cookies after my ride."

"All right, sweetie."

Jason patted his sister's hand lovingly. "You get your rest, my dear. I'll see you after Laurel finishes showing me around." With a wan smile, Clair followed Taylor and Brooke toward the house.

"The horses are over here, Mr. Portland," Laurel said sweetly. Lifting the edge of her skirt to keep it from getting soiled, she stepped into the barn. She was giddy at the thought of being alone with Jason, even for a few minutes.

Walking slowly down the aisle, she showed him each of the horses. They scared her a little. Laurel could ride but not as well as Taylor and Kendra. She always felt a little too out of control when she sat atop the tall animals.

At the far end of the barn was the stallion, Ward Marston's pride and joy.

"He's beautiful, Laurel. I can see why your uncle is so proud of him."

"I was so pleased to receive your sister's letter about your visit to Catawba," Laurel ventured to remark. Unused to being alone with a man, she wasn't quite sure what to say.

"My sister missed you terribly after you left England. When she received your first letter, it was all she talked about for days. As it turns out, she has been making plans to come visit you for some time, and since she couldn't come unchaperoned, I took it upon myself to escort her."

"What do you think of Catawba?"

"It's very pleasant. A little primitive, perhaps, compared to England, but it has potential. With the right person handling the affairs, I'm sure Catawba could become one of the largest plantations around."

"That's what my father would like. Uncle Ward doesn't care about that. He just wants to raise horses and sell lumber." Realizing that her words made Ward sound weak, Laurel quickly added, "Don't get me wrong, he's a hard worker and wants the best for the family, but he says wealth and position are not what's important here in America."

"Your uncle sounds like a typical American. I think he's been here too long. Take his workers, for instance. Half of them are free. That's no good—you need the structure of classes in order for everybody to know his place."

Taken aback by his words, Laurel was silent. She knew it wouldn't be right to argue with Jason, but neither did she believe those things anymore. Even her father was beginning to change his views. Quickly reverting to a lady's ploy for avoiding a difficult topic, Laurel played ignorant.

"Well, I'm sure you men know what we need. You're so much better at coping with those things than women." She batted her eyes slowly, keeping her expression blank and her lips smiling.

Jason puffed out his chest proudly. "Yes, my dear, it would probably be better to let the men handle such things. We've been taking good care of the women for quite some time."

Jason lifted Laurel's slender hand and brushed his lips lightly across the knuckles. "I want you to know, Laurel, that Clair's need for an escort was not the only reason I came here. After you left England I found that I missed your beauty and enjoyable humor."

Laurel's mouth dropped open in surprise. She tried to gather her scrambled thoughts.

"I . . . uh . . . I don't know what to say," she mumbled.

"Don't say anything. Let us just spend time together and get to know each other again."

Squeezing her hand, Jason pulled it through the crook of his arm, and they walked out the barn door and into the sunlight. As they paused for a moment to let their eyes adjust, Laurel turned toward the house. Her hand flew to her throat in surprise. Joshua Douglas stood in front of them.

He looked magnificent. His long legs were enclosed in buff breeches and tall black boots. A linen shirt hung loosely, billowing slightly in the breeze. His dark hair was pulled into a sleek tail. Laurel was unable to tear her eyes away from him.

Joshua didn't seem to be suffering from the same problem. "Good afternoon, Miss Marston," he greeted her stiffly.

"Mr. Douglas." Laurel continued to stare until Joshua's glance shifted to Jason. Embarrassed by her lack of manners, she turned a flushed face to Jason.

"Mr. Douglas, I would like to introduce you to Jason Portland. He and his sister are here to visit us for awhile. Mr. Portland, this is Joshua Douglas, a neighbor." She watched as the two men shook hands.

Next to Joshua's tall, dark frame, Jason looked pale and small. His manicured hand seemed almost feminine in Joshua's work-hardened grasp. *They are as different as night and day*, Laurel thought, and shifted uncomfortably from foot to foot. No one knew that Joshua had kissed her, but Laurel felt as if anyone could tell from the way they were sizing each other up.

"You are a neighbor to Catawba, Mr. Douglas?"

"Yes, that's right." Dark-blue eyes met light-blue in a challenging stare.

Anxious to get back to the house, Laurel nervously spoke up. "Was there something you needed, Mr. Douglas?"

His gaze shifted to Laurel, roaming casually over her face. The smile on his lips didn't reach his eyes.

"I've come to see your sister. I heard she had an accident yesterday, and I wanted to see for myself that she was all right."

"I can assure you that Kendra is recovering satisfactorily. Thank you for asking." Laurel stood rigidly. Joshua Douglas had humiliated her, but she would not allow him to do the same thing to Kendra. She would protect her sister from this man.

Joshua smiled mockingly and bowed. "If I have your permission, Miss Marston, I think I'll see Kendra for myself. Mr. Portland, it was," he hesitated, "a pleasure to meet you." He turned toward the house, paused, and turned back.

"Oh, by the way, Miss Marston, I forgot to thank you for a most enjoyable time in the swamp the other evening. It was . . . quite memorable." With an insolent grin, he continued on his way.

Sputtering in agitation, Laurel briefly forgot that she wasn't alone. "Oh, that horrible, horrible man!" she muttered, staring after him. "I'd like to wring his neck! I'd like to . . . like to. . . ." Her anger drained away as she was suddenly consumed with the memory of her fingers running through his hair and the feel of his arms crushing her close as he kissed her.

She didn't see the sudden rage on Jason's face as he watched her stare at the retreating back of Joshua Douglas. She was trying desperately to regain her composure. She felt betrayed by her own thoughts as she turned back. "I apologize for that man, sir. Mr. Douglas, I have found, is no gentleman."

Jason had quickly schooled his face to its usual pleasantness. "It's quite all right, my dear. I wouldn't expect these American barbarians to possess the qualities of a gentleman. The stories I've heard about their lack of manners have been confirmed." Together, they proceeded back to the house, where he bowed slightly over her hand.

"If you would excuse me. I am concerned after my sister's health."

Laurel stood at the bottom of the steps, watching Jason ascend. His manners were perfect. He stood when she entered a room. He had escorted her to the noon meal. He lavished his attention on her, continually praising her beauty. She had spent an enjoyable afternoon in the company of a fine gentleman. That was how Laurel wanted to spend the rest of her life. Not with an unmannerly rake like Joshua Douglas.

Yet, if that were truly how she felt, then why did her traitorous heart leap at the mere sight of Joshua? Surely that wasn't love . . . was it? Marissa Ferguson had told Laurel that sometimes people were attracted to each other physically, but that it wasn't always love. Was that what she was feeling?

Laurel sighed. She was so confused. She knew that when she chose a man in marriage, it would be for a lifetime. She wanted to make the right decision. Could she?

Her stomach growled, reminding her of more mundane things. Remembering Brooke's mention of cookies, she made her way around the back of the house to find Taylor and Brooke having a snack outside the kitchen door.

"Do you mind having some company?" she asked as she approached.

Taylor glanced up, looking over Laurel's shoulder. Jason Portland wasn't there. She gladly offered Laurel a seat.

Seating herself, Laurel came to a decision. "Aunt Taylor, do you mind if I ask you a question?"

"Of course not."

"What made you fall in love with Uncle Ward?" Laurel wasn't sure what she wanted to hear, but she hoped the older woman's answer would help.

"That's a big question." Taylor thought a moment before answering. "I think the biggest thing was that he was a Christian and had such high morals. It's so important to find someone who is good and kind. If he treats others fairly, then he'll treat his family fairly." She laughed. "Of course, his incredible good looks were a bonus." Laurel didn't respond to her teasing, and Taylor looked inquiringly at her. "Why do you ask?"

Laurel shrugged, not willing to say. "I was just curious." Then, remembering Marissa's words about respect, she hesitantly asked, "What about respect? Is that important in a marriage? Does Uncle Ward respect you?"

"Respect isn't automatic—it has to be earned. If a person is trustworthy and a man of his word, then it comes naturally. Respect is a big part of love. In a marriage, a husband needs to know his wife is going to be there for him, to encourage and lift him up when needed. And vice versa. And, yes, I do believe your uncle respects me."

Laurel was relieved. "But do other marriages have that kind of respect?"

"Unfortunately, not always. That's why it's important to be sure of whom you're marrying. You need to look beyond the surface and see what type of man he really is."

"Should a wife allow her husband to kiss other women if that's what he wants?" Laurel knew she was stepping onto shaky ground, but she wanted to get her questions answered.

Taylor gave Laurel a quizzical look. "A lot of women have to put up with that. Some husbands don't want only one woman. But it's certainly not a godly attitude."

"What would you do if Uncle Ward kissed another woman?"

Taylor gasped. "I don't know, Laurel. I'd be very hurt. But I don't think your Uncle Ward is like that. He's an honest man and would never go against God's Word."

Laurel knew Taylor was right. Why Marissa had ever said those things about her Uncle Ward, Laurel didn't know, but she had no doubt that the other girl had lied. Relieved of most of her anxieties, she reached for a cookie.

Taylor looked fondly at her niece. She could tell that Laurel had a lot of things on her mind. Things that most young women went through at some point in their lives. Love was both a wonderful and a frightening prospect. Taylor hoped that her niece would be guided toward the right answers—and the right man. She didn't press Laurel for details, but let cookies and milk soothe the young woman's troubled heart.

Jason knocked lightly on the door and stepped in. Clair was sitting up in bed. He closed the door carefully behind him.

"Oh, Jason," Clair exclaimed. "Did I do it right? Was I too obvious?"

"You did fine, my dear."

"Are you sure?" she asked beseechingly.

"Clair, everything is fine. Please don't worry yourself." Jason patted his sister's shoulder, then paced around the room. "I need you to do something for me."

Eagerly, Clair listened. "Anything. Just tell me what it is."

Jason smiled fondly at his sister. Clair was such a dainty creature. Most people didn't realize how truly fragile she was, how tiny and delicate her bones. But he did.

Clair had been the one who actually started Jason thinking about America. He had recently discovered that his financial standings were crumbling, and he'd been desperate for a solution. When his sister started talking about Laurel Marston, Jason could barely remember what she looked like. But who cared? What had caught his interest was the mention of Catawba. Laurel's letters gave vivid details of how it was growing and prospering—prospering so well that Jason took it upon himself to learn more about the Marston family.

After some digging, he found what he wanted. The Marstons were quite wealthy, and Catawba was making a name for itself in the American South. Laurel would stand to make a great deal of money from her father and uncle. He had the perfect situation falling right into his hands.

Jason began making plans immediately. Using the last of their money, he and Clair made the trip to America. She was going to visit Laurel. He was going to marry her.

What girl in her right mind would turn down an influential Englishman? It didn't matter that his family was nearly penniless. He still had his titles and lands. And his looks. Jason was well aware of the effect he had on women. He was counting on that to win Laurel Marston's hand and money in marriage.

Jason returned his thoughts to the present. "There's a neighbor who might cause a problem with my plan. I want you to find out everything about him."

Frowning, Clair cocked her head. "What kind of problem? Does he wish to marry Laurel as well?"

"I'm not sure. But after all the plans we've made I wouldn't want him to interfere." Jason gazed out the window. His eyes glittered with anger. *This has to work or there will be nothing left,* he thought. *It will work.*

"What's his name?"

"Joshua Douglas." Smoothing his features, he turned. "I believe Mr. Douglas is visiting with Kendra. Maybe it would be a good time for you to get a little information."

"Oh," Clair looked down at her rumpled gown. "My dress is too wrinkled. I couldn't possibly meet him without making myself more presentable. It might take quite a while."

Stepping to her side, Joshua gave his sister a quick hug. "My dear, you look beautiful. No man would even take notice of your gown."

Clair flushed prettily at his praise. "Very well. I'll find out as much as I can about this man."

"Thank you. Clair? You will be happy when I marry Laurel Marston, won't you?"

"Oh, yes, Jason. I think she's perfect for you."

"As do I. Now run along and find out everything you can."

"Yes, Jason," Clair said obediently.

Removing the bandage from Kendra's head, Maida inspected the wound closely. The left side of her forehead was an ugly mass of purples and greens, but the cut was healing properly, which was a good sign.

"I think you could sit on the porch to visit with Mr. Douglas if you'd like," Maida said, pleased with Kendra's recovery. "Fresh air would be good for you right now."

Tossing back the covers, Kendra almost leaped from the bed. A restraining hand from Maida held her back.

"You just told me I could go downstairs."

"Yes, but you're not to walk on your own. Your Uncle Ward will be up shortly to bring you down." Reaching into the wardrobe, Maida pulled out a day dress. "I'll help you dress."

Kendra's lower lip stuck out, and Maida laughed. "You are not going to heal properly if you don't give your body time." She paused. "You've only been in bed one day. We could always keep you here in the room."

"No!" yelped Kendra.

Smiling fondly down at her charge, Maida smoothed her hair away from her face. "We want to pamper you a little, Kendra. Give us a chance to take care of you."

"All right," Kendra conceded.

Sitting on the edge of the bed, Kendra allowed Maida to help her dress and within moments was scooped into Ward's arms and carried down to the large porch. Seating her in a comfortable, plush chair, a carpet over her knees, he bowed mockingly.

"Is there anything more I can do for your majesty?"

Giggling happily, Kendra shook her head. "Thank you, Uncle Ward." He leaned down and kissed her on the cheek.

"I'll see you later, little Kendra."

Kendra closed her eyes and leaned back in the chair, letting the sun warm her face. It felt good to be outside. She sighed, breathing in the fresh air.

"Kendra."

The voice startled Kendra alert. She opened her eyes to see Court standing below in the yard.

"Court," she whispered. The memory of their last meeting seared her heart.

"How are you feeling?" He held his hat in hand, nervously twisted the brim.

"Fine."

"I'm glad to hear that."

"I love you, Court," Kendra said quietly.

Hopelessness filled Court's eyes. "I hope you find someone who will make you happy, Kendra. I'm not right for you." Turning, he strode away.

Tears trickled down Kendra's cheeks. She didn't bother to wipe them away. In fact, it was a relief to release them. Deflated and miserable, she sat alone on the porch. The day had lost its brightness.

"I hope that glum look isn't because you saw me coming." Joshua stood in the doorway watching Kendra intently. She wiped at her tears.

"Actually I didn't see you there, Mr. Douglas."

"Joshua. After all the time we've spent together I think it would be appropriate if you called me Joshua." Sitting in a chair near Kendra, he leaned closer. "You want to tell someone your troubles? I'm a good listener."

Kendra did wish she could talk to someone. No one in her family would understand, she was sure of that. Maybe an outsider would be able to help. But could she trust Joshua? She still had no clue as to whom Lizy belonged. Was he the cruel master?

"Kendra," Joshua said, gently taking her hand. "Sometimes it helps to talk about your problems. It might give you a better perspective. You may even find they don't seem so bad afterward." He smiled encouragingly and before Kendra could think about it, she was telling him everything, from the moment she met Court Yardley until today. She would have never thought it possible to talk about such things with a man, but she was bursting, and Joshua had caught her at the right moment.

"Well," said Joshua after Kendra had poured everything out. "It sounds to me like your Mr. Yardley is a little jealous of our time together. I'm sure he still loves you. He just feels unworthy of you."

"Do you think so?"

"No man could declare his love like that and then just turn it off. Being a man myself, I know what I'm talking about. So take heart. But if I may offer a little advice . . . ?" She nodded. "Pray for guidance, Kendra. Ask God to show you what would be best."

"You're a Christian, Joshua?" Kendra was surprised. She had never thought to ask him. *Surely a Christian wouldn't abuse slaves*, she thought hopefully.

"Yes."

Chewing the inside of her lip, Kendra frowned. "Are you a *good* Christian?" she asked tentatively.

"I hope so." He looked puzzled. "Why do you ask?"

"Oh, you know how people like to talk when there's a new person in the area. Just idle gossip." Maybe now was the time to find out the truth. She changed tactics.

"Have things been going well at your farm?"

"Yes, quite well."

"Father is always complaining about the slaves. Do you own slaves, Joshua?" Kendra held her breath in anticipation.

"Yes, I own a few slaves. But not as many as your father." Stretching out his legs, Joshua leaned back comfortably.

"Have you heard about the runaway slave girl that was being hunted in the area?"

"Yes, as a matter of fact. She belonged to me."

"She did?" Kendra squeaked.

Joshua nodded. "That's what my overseer told me."

Kendra frowned. "You didn't know anything about it?"

"No. The farm had been running for almost six months before I moved in. My overseer ran the entire operation and only contacted me if there were any problems. This was the first one I'd ever heard of."

Relief washed over Kendra. "Oh, Joshua, I'm so glad to hear that."

"Why?" He eyed her curiously.

"Because I like you, and I hated to think you might be a cruel master to your slaves. Even though my father owns slaves, he treats them well, and they can raise families without fear of being sold."

"That's a good plan."

"What about the girl?" Kendra asked hesitantly.

Joshua shrugged. "There's not much I can do. She ran away, so she'll be tracked and brought back."

"What if there was a reason for why she ran?"

"Like what?" asked Joshua, suddenly more interested in the conversation.

"What would you do if you found she had been beaten? And that was the reason she ran away. You couldn't really blame her for that, could you?" Kendra pleaded.

"Is that what happened, Kendra?" he asked intently.

Nodding vigorously, Kendra's throat constricted in fear. Was her desire to help Lizy clouding her judgment? She couldn't betray Taylor. Yet, if Joshua didn't even know who the girl was, someone else must have beaten her.

Joshua was watching Kendra closely. "You thought it was me, didn't you?"

Again Kendra nodded.

"What about the girl?"

"Maybe . . . maybe she would come back if she knew she'd be safe." Joshua stared at her thoughtfully, then nodded.

"I'll look into the problem at the farm and let you know when it's been taken care of." The look in his eye promised immediate action. Kendra was glad that she wasn't his overseer.

"Am I interrupting anything?" Clair Portland asked, stepping onto the porch.

Rising to his feet, Joshua bowed over her extended hand. Kendra rolled her eyes. Clair Portland was the silliest, weakest girl she'd ever met.

"Clair Portland, I'd like to introduce Joshua Douglas. Joshua, this is Clair Portland from England."

"Would you like to join us?" Joshua offered. "An afternoon spent in the company of two beautiful ladies would be a great pleasure."

Giggling behind her hand, Clair took a seat near Kendra. "Please don't let me interrupt your conversation."

"We were just finishing," Joshua said gallantly. "How was your journey from England?"

"Oh, it was dreadful. The seas were so rough. I didn't dare leave my cabin." Clair's hand fluttered through the air in agitation. Kendra had to bite the inside of her mouth to stop her irritated words. She couldn't abide weak women.

"Well you're safe on land now," soothed Joshua.

"Yes, but the trip here to Catawba was even worse. There was no place to sleep except in the wagon. The roads were so rough I was sure I'd never stop jiggling and bouncing." Enjoying the attention, Clair continued her story of their journey.

An hour later, Kendra tried to hold back the yawn that threatened to crack her jaw. Clair had been talking to Joshua non-stop. After describing her journey, she'd asked about his farm. Kendra enjoyed hearing Joshua's stories, but Clair made an irritating trill every time his story got a bit descriptive.

"I think it's time for Miss Kendra to return to her room," remarked Joshua, noticing the concealed yawn. "You've been out here long enough." He stood and leaned over to lift Kendra.

"Would you be so kind as to direct me to your room."

Kendra gave him a broad smile and directed him up the stairs with Clair following them quietly. Bowing over Kendra's hand, Joshua placed a small kiss on her knuckles.

"Sleep well, Kendra. I will come visit you again another day." He and Clair left the room and went down.

"It was a pleasure, Miss Portland."

"I look forward to seeing you again, Mr. Douglas."

Clair couldn't remember the last time she'd enjoyed an afternoon so much. She was glad Jason had asked her to spend time with Mr. Douglas. He was a perfect gentleman, and the stories he told were so exciting.

Hoping the information she'd gleaned that afternoon would make Jason happy, Clair went in search of her brother.

As he rode back to his farm, Joshua thought over his conversation with Kendra. She had raised some serious questions, and he was determined to get to the bottom of things. He didn't know just what was going on, but perhaps Matthew would have some answers. The older man kept abreast of everything—it amused him to keep up the image of an excellent servant even though he was Joshua's closest friend.

Joshua didn't like being left in the dark about his own farm. And, if true, this would be a big problem. Kendra said that the runaway girl had been abused, and the only one with the authority to do that was the overseer. And if so. . . . His jaw tightened as he galloped into his yard and jumped from the saddle. Tossing the reins to the waiting stable boy, he marched into the house.

"Matthew," he bellowed. "Where are you?"

"Right here, sir," came the voice of his friend. Matthew appeared in the hallway. Joshua gestured for Matthew to follow him into his office and closed the door firmly behind him.

"I need some information, Matthew."

"Anything I know, sir, I'll be glad to tell you." The dark-skinned man waited calmly.

"What can you tell me about my slaves being beaten?"

Without flicking an eyelash, Matthew told Joshua, in detail, all that had been happening behind Joshua's back. With each word that the old man spoke, Joshua's heart grew heavier. He clenched and unclenched his fists as he paced the room.

"Is that all?" he demanded.

"Yes, sir."

"Why didn't anyone tell me this before?"

"Your overseer has gone to great pains to hide his abuse. If you had confronted him, he would have denied it, stopped for a short time until you were no longer suspicious, and then taken it out on the slaves. He's very careful to keep from excessively marking them, so you would not have known. And they are afraid of what he will do to their families, so they would not speak. Your information must have come from someone outside this house, from someone other than your workers. Now you will believe what you never see."

Joshua slammed his fist into his hand, his mind reeling with the horror of what Matthew had just told him. That that man had *dared* to abuse his people. . . . He wheeled to Matthew.

"The first thing we need to do is get rid of the overseer. Then I want to speak to all the slaves. They need to know that they'll be treated fairly from now on. Families will stay together as long as they work. I give my word on that. Now, you gather the workers in front of the house. I," his eyes gleamed, "have an overseer to sack."

Jerking the door open, Joshua marched out of the office. The next few minutes were going to be very pleasurable.

Some hours later found Joshua grinning as he returned to the house. His former overseer would think twice about showing his face in these parts for some time to come. Joshua had given him a thorough verbal lashing and booted him off his land. Several of the slaves had been standing nearby when he'd dismissed the man. He had taken the opportunity to let them know they would be safe to raise their families without fear of sale or abuse. Not a sound had come from the scruffy group, but he had sensed the relief. Now all he had to do was see Kendra about the return of his runaway slave girl. He would visit her again tomorrow to discuss the plans.

Joshua lowered himself into a chair and relaxed. The afternoon at Catawba had been very interesting. Clair Portland was a sweet child, but a complete bore. He smiled. It was obvious that Kendra was of the same opinion. When he'd caught her hiding a yawn, he'd grabbed at the chance for a graceful exit.

And then there was Clair's brother. Joshua's eyes narrowed. When Laurel had introduced the two men, Joshua had had to fight the urge to pound the English dandy into the ground. What did Laurel see in that peacock? She deserved better. Against his will, he thought about the day he had kissed her. More than anything, he had wanted to take her back into his arms and kiss her senseless. She had stood there glaring at him today, and all Joshua had been able to think of was that he had never seen anyone so beautiful.

He didn't know what the future held, but one thing was certain. Seeing Jason Portland touching Laurel had tied his stomach into knots.

"What have you found out?" questioned Jason.

"He's an interesting man. We had a very nice conversation. He told me all about his farm." Clair didn't notice the effect her words were having on Jason.

"I don't care what kind of conversationalist he is, Clair," Jason said through gritted teeth. "What did you find out about him."

"He came to South Carolina to build a home. Trapping and tracking is what he did before. He's traveled a great deal and seen a lot of this country, but now he's ready to settle down and start a family."

"Is that all?" Jason asked stiffly.

"Well, I'm sure there was more, but we talked for so long I don't remember everything." Clair's blue eyes filled with tears. "Was that not enough, Jason? Maybe I could learn more from Kendra or Laurel."

"No," Jason whispered fiercely. "If you could not do the job properly the first time, why should I trust you again?"

"I know I could do better, Jason," she pleaded. "Please give me another chance."

Shaking his head, Jason turned his back on his sister. "No, Clair. You're no good to me like this."

She came to his side and put a hand on his arm. "I'm sorry. Please, Jason. I want to make you happy." Her head dropped when he remained silent, her tears falling. Finally he spoke.

"Very well, Clair. I will give you one more chance. But I warn you, do not disappoint me again." His voice was so low that Clair had to strain to hear his words.

"Thank you, Jason. I promise to do better."

Clair had been given a reprieve. Now she had to get the information Jason wanted. She had borne the brunt of his temper many times in the past, and she had no wish to endure it now.

When he was younger, Jason had been very charming. But when he found that their father had squandered all their money, he'd begun to change. It had started small—things like squeezing Clair's arm until it bruised. But it hadn't stopped there. The more worried Jason became about their financial situation, the more he took it out on Clair. She took the blame for everything. She couldn't fight her brother, so she endured his abuse. There was nothing she could do about it until she married and moved away. She dreamed of that day.

Learning of Jason's interest in Laurel Marston had been a surprise. Clair hadn't realized he listened to her talk about her friend. She tried not to feel guilty for thinking that if he married Laurel, then maybe he would be happy and not hurt her anymore.

It wasn't until the next morning that Kendra was able to have a moment alone with Taylor to tell her about the conversation she'd had with Joshua.

Taylor gasped in alarm. "You told Joshua Douglas about Lizy? Kendra, how could you?" Taylor tried to think quickly. *They've already looked for the girl once and didn't't find her. But if they think she's here, will they search more thoroughly?*

"Aunt Taylor, listen to me," pleaded Kendra. "He's not the one who did it. It was the overseer. Joshua barely knew the girl had run away."

"But, Kendra, you've put us all in danger even by hinting that you knew where she was. You can't do that."

"Joshua promised to deal with the problem at the farm. Then we can figure out what to do with Lizy."

Taylor sat down heavily in the chair near the bed. "I have been more nervous about this girl than any of the others we've helped."

"We? Who else is helping you?"

Taylor tried to cover up her words. "I was only thinking of you and me when I said that."

"Tell me, Aunt Taylor. Who's helping you?" Taylor's eyes dropped.

Kendra's eyes narrowed. She quickly made a mental list of possible helpers. It wouldn't be Laurel. She was too proper to get involved in something so dangerous. It certainly was not her father. Knowing his views on slavery, Kendra was fairly certain he would be furious if he knew the farm was being used as a safehouse. Reid? Too young. Ward? Possibly, since Taylor said he knew about Lizy, but Kendra didn't think he'd have the time to do anything illegal since he was busy morning to night with the plantation. Court? She paused. He *was* always around, and Kendra knew he hated slavery. She slowly stiffened as she realized that Court was the most logical answer.

"It's Court, isn't it?" she asked quietly, her face losing color.

Taylor couldn't meet Kendra's eyes. She had promised Court never to reveal his secret, but Kendra had guessed it. "Listen to me, Kendra. You have to forget about this."

"Forget about it?" Her head was spinning, but Kendra ignored it as her thoughts focused on Court. "He's been helping runaways all this time and not once told me about it!"

"Why would he tell you?" Taylor asked, confused.

Turning hurt, angry eyes on Taylor, Kendra burst out, "Because he said he loved me, that's why. If he couldn't trust me with this, then how can I believe he really cares about me?"

"Court loves you?" Taylor was amazed.

Hysterical laughter rose in Kendra's throat. "Not anymore, it seems."

Taylor gripped Kendra's arm. "Now listen to me, Kendra. I don't know about your relationship with Court. But I do know that he had to keep this secret. If it had ever been discovered that he was helping runaways, the entire family could have been in jeopardy."

"It doesn't matter anyway," Kendra said. "Even now that I know the truth, it doesn't matter. Court has turned his back on our love and refuses to acknowledge it." Her shoulders drooped.

Taylor took her back over to the bed. "If Court truly loves you, nothing he says or does can change that. I'm sure that everything will work out fine."

"He thought I was in love with Joshua Douglas," Kendra filled in.

"I see. Then you'll just have to convince him that you won't stop caring about him."

"But how?"

"People who have been hurt try to protect themselves from further pain. You'll have to break through the barrier Court has probably built around his heart. Make him see all the love you say you have for him."

Wiping away her tears, Kendra smiled weakly. "You're the best, Aunt Taylor. Thank you." She hesitated. "You won't tell anyone about this, will you?"

Cammie knocked on the door and entered. "Excuse me. Miss Kendra, Mr. Douglas is waiting to see you downstairs."

"Good." Rising from the bed, Kendra started out the door.

"Are you sure about this, Kendra?" Taylor's simple question halted her. The concern in her aunt's voice was frightening and she realized what hung in the balance. All it would take was Joshua Douglas relating what Kendra had told him to the authorities and they would all be arrested. She tried to act confident.

"I've spent a lot of time with Joshua, Aunt Taylor. He's a good man; I know it. I would trust him with my life."

Taylor nodded. "Very well."

After Kendra left, Cammie searched Taylor's face. "I think Miss Kendra be right. Don't be afraid, Miss Taylor."

"I'm trying very hard not to be, Cammie." Not wanting to dwell on the possibilities, Taylor rose. She had a strong urge to see Ward. She needed his strength.

"Cammie, do you know where Ward is?"

"Down in the barn, Miss Taylor."

"Would you go to the kitchen and pack us a picnic basket? I'm going to see if I can kidnap my husband for the afternoon."

Cammie smiled at her mistress. "I surely will, Miss Taylor."

"Ward, are you in here?" Taylor called soon after, stepping into the barn.

"Over here, Taylor," he called back.

Glancing up toward the loft, Taylor found him shirtless, with a pitchfork in hand. "Are you busy?" she asked.

"I'm never too busy for you, my love,"

Taylor set the basket of food down and headed for the wooden ladder. Glancing to make sure no one was around, she scooped her skirts up high and climbed into the loft.

Ward was waiting for her at the top, arms outstretched. "May I be of service, my lady?"

"I have come to fetch you for an afternoon of frolicking."

"Sounds very interesting," Ward said, raising his eyebrows.

"I have a basket full of food and a desire to go into the woods with my husband. What do you say?"

Ward grabbed his linen shirt and tossed it over his head. "Lead the way, wife."

As they walked toward the trees, Taylor congratulated herself on her good advice. She loved Ward with all her heart and thanked God daily that she was married to him. Having both him and Brooke made her life complete. *Would it really be so awful if we never have any more children?* she wondered.

"Ward, do you want more children?"

"Are you expecting?" Ward asked excitedly.

Taylor shook her head. "No, I'm just asking."

Ward didn't answer right away. "I would like more children, but it's not so important to me that I'd be unhappy without them. You and Brooke are all I need." Pulling

Taylor into his arms, Ward tried to kiss her but she pushed him away.

"I want to talk about this, please."

"Aren't we talking?"

"Please, Ward."

Seeing that she was serious, he sobered instantly. Taylor continued.

"You wouldn't mind if I never gave you a son?"

"No."

"Don't you feel a little envious of Yates and Maida?"

"No."

Taylor's exasperated sigh brought Ward to a stop. "What's this all about? You say you're not expecting, so what's the problem?"

"I want to have a baby," she almost yelled in frustration. "But I don't think I can."

Ward finally understood. He took Taylor into his arms. "Taylor, I love you and I love Brooke. You're my family. If we never have any more children, I'll still be happy. That won't change the way I feel about you. You're my wife forever."

"You don't regret marrying me, then."

"How could I regret the smartest move in my life?" Ward tried to hold her, but Taylor wanted to clear everything up. It was now or never and she was tired of living with jealous thoughts of Marissa Ferguson stealing her husband away.

"If you were given the chance to pick anyone around here for a wife—who would you choose?"

Ward frowned. The question was so absurd, he wasn't sure what to say. He wasn't sure what Taylor *wanted* him to say. He eyed her warily. "Is there someone you have in mind?"

Taylor shrugged. "Is there someone *you* have in mind?"

"Taylor," Ward sighed in exasperation, "you're the only woman I'm interested in. I love you. No one else—just you. Now come here and show me how much you love me."

Leaping at her husband, Taylor tumbled him to the ground, where they fell in a laughing heap. *He loves me*, she thought. *He loves me*. She rolled on top of him, raining little kisses all over his face. With each one, she said she loved him.

Ward didn't view their lack of children as a failure. She should have known better. She couldn't help thinking, though, as she kissed her husband, *Marissa Ferguson can find her own man and leave mine alone!*

Kendra found Joshua waiting for her in the front parlor and nervously stepped in. She had reassured Taylor about trusting the man, but a glimmer of doubt at her own judgment made her hesitate. Joshua's smiling face erased her apprehension immediately.

"Kendra, good morning." Coming forward, he glanced at her wound before escorting her to a seat. "How are you feeling this morning?"

"I'm fine, Joshua. It looks worse than it feels."

"I'm glad to hear that." Lowering his voice, he whispered, "The problem at my home has been taken care of. My people won't be abused any longer and they'll be allowed to raise their families in peace."

"Oh, Joshua," Kendra clutched at his hand. "That's good news."

"Now, we only have to solve your little, ahem, guest problem and everything will be all right."

"What can we do? I don't think she'll go willingly. She's too frightened."

"Do you think she'd talk to me?" Joshua suggested.

"I don't know. We wouldn't be able to do anything until dark. I'll ask about it and let you know." Kendra still hadn't told Joshua about Taylor's involvement and definitely not about Court's. She winced inwardly. Knowing Court's mistrust of her was still too painful.

"Send me a message, and I'll return this evening."

"Very well."

Joshua stood. "I must go now. There's a lot of work to be done, and without an overseer, I'll have to do it myself." He grinned down at Kendra. "Goodbye, Miss Marston."

"Good day to you, Mr. Douglas." Kendra giggled. To anyone half listening, their conversation would have appeared normal.

Seeing Joshua out, Kendra went in search of Taylor. There was work to be done before this evening if Lizy was to be returned to her home. She was dismayed to find that her aunt had disappeared with Ward for the day. That left only one other person she could talk to—Court. She sighed. It wouldn't be easy, but she had to find out what to do about Lizy.

Father God, she prayed, *help me do this. Help me remember how I'm helping Lizy*. Kendra went in search of Court.

Finding him was easy, getting him to talk to her was not. Kendra leaned against the corral rails, watching Court put a horse through her paces. *He's good with horses*, she thought proudly. She caught his eye and waved him toward her. He paused before riding over to look down at her. The sun shone behind his back.

"What can I do for you, Miss Marston?"

"I need to speak with you about an urgent matter, Court." Kendra squinted up at him.

"I'm in the middle of training. Can it not wait?" Court didn't want to speak with Kendra. He knew it wasn't right to refuse her request, but he couldn't trust himself to stay away from her.

"Mr. Yardley, this is an urgent matter. I can assure you it has nothing to do about you and me. So if you would kindly get down off that horse, I would appreciate it."

Court glanced around sharply to make sure no one had heard her. Embarrassed at his own reluctance, he slid from the mare's back, holding the reins in his hand. "What can I do for you, Miss Marston?"

"I have spoken with my Aunt Taylor and have deduced that you've been helping her with runaways." Kendra paused, letting the full import of her words sink in. Court's mouth opened and closed several times. "I'm not going to tell you how it hurt me, knowing you couldn't trust me with that information. Nor am I going to remind you that, had anything ever happened to you because of helping them, I wouldn't have been able to help you because of my ignorance." Court's eyes narrowed, but Kendra overrode him.

"What I am going to tell you is that Joshua Douglas owns Lizy. It was his overseer who beat her. Mr. Douglas has taken care of the problem. He wants the chance to talk to Lizy and see if she's willing to come back to his farm. Since Aunt Taylor isn't around, I had to come to you for suggestions."

Kendra stopped, out of breath. It wasn't easy standing here with Court, knowing that he no longer wanted her. Even if his motivations of jealously were unfounded, it didn't change the fact that he'd turned away from her when she'd sworn her love for him. But she refused to show her hurt and faced Court calmly.

Court was dumbfounded at her words. "How do you know about Lizy?" he asked suspiciously.

"I'm the one who found her." Lifting her chin, Kendra dared him to make any judgment.

"And you're angry with me?" Court stared at her disbelievingly. "Are you out of your mind? Do you know how dangerous all of this is? I don't remember you telling me about your part in this little situation. Didn't you trust me, Kendra?" He frowned at her angrily.

Court's words stung. Kendra hadn't thought about the consequences of keeping her involvement from him. What a mess. She hadn't said anything in order to protect him and he hadn't said anything in order to protect her. Her anger dissipated.

"I'm sorry, Court. I wasn't thinking."

Court stared at her stonily and then sighed, shaking his head. "It doesn't matter, Kendra."

"Yes, it does." Desperation gave her words strength. She leaned over the railing that separated them. "It does matter. I should have told you. I was wrong. Please forgive me."

Court's face contorted in pain. "It doesn't matter." He emphasized each word carefully. "Not any more. You're no longer beholden to me, Kendra."

"But Court, I love you. Doesn't that mean anything to you anymore?" Her head was beginning to ache again, but she ignored it. This was the last time she'd humiliate herself in front of Court. If he turned her away this time, she'd let him go—for good.

"It means the world to me, Kendra, but it doesn't change anything. You need a fine, upstanding gentleman.

We both know that'll never be me. You deserve the best," Court ended on a whisper.

Slowly Kendra stepped off of the railing. With hollow eyes, she stood a picture of dejection. "I'll wait to see what Aunt Taylor says about Lizy," she said tonelessly. "Don't worry, Mr. Yardley, you won't have to turn me down ever again."

Without another word, she returned to the house and her room, throwing herself across the bed and waiting for the tears to come. Nothing happened. She was empty inside. She had given everything to Court and had nothing for herself.

Kendra refused all contact with her family for the rest of the afternoon. She didn't want to see anyone. She didn't want to speak to anyone. It wasn't until Taylor returned late in the day that she finally opened up her door. She'd promised Joshua the chance to speak with Lizy and somehow she would see that he did. She told Taylor the bare facts and let her aunt deal with the problem.

After much persuasion, Lizy had agreed to see Joshua and a messenger had been sent to the Douglas farm inviting him for supper. He would see Lizy after dark. Not in the saferoom, though. Not even Joshua could know about that secret. He arrived that evening and was escorted to the parlor where everyone waited for supper.

"Joshua, it's good of you to join us." Ward shook his hand. "How are things over your way?"

"As well as can be expected. The place was so run down that it's taking longer than expected to get it back on its feet." Joshua slowly surveyed the room, stopping briefly on Laurel. She was sitting next to Jason Portland. Joshua frowned.

"Well, come on in and sit down. Dinner will be ready shortly."

Greetings came from the rest. Laurel's was a little stiff and Jason Portland's was covertly hostile. *Interesting*, decided Joshua. Taylor and Kendra smiled at him from across the room. Clair Portland's enthusiastic greeting included an invitation to seat himself beside her, and he accepted.

Conversation flowed around the room. It was a new experience for Joshua, finding himself in the middle of a large family. They seemed to enjoy each other's company and their remarks were punctuated with teasing and laughter. A deep ache started gnawing at Joshua's insides. This is what he had been looking for, he realized. A family—people who lived and loved and worked together. As a child, he'd never had the chance for something like this, and he ached for it now. The Marstons were good people, and he was grateful to be a part of them, even if it wasn't forever. His eyes found Laurel.

"Dinner is served," a servant called from the doorway, interrupting Joshua's reflection. The informal party broke up as everyone stood and Ward and Yates escorted their wives from the room. As Jason took Laurel's arm, he flashed a look of triumph at Joshua. Laurel kept her eyes down as she passed by.

Joshua turned to Clair and Kendra. "Well, I have the distinct pleasure of escorting not one, but two lovely ladies to dinner tonight. I should visit more often." He was rewarded with two brilliant smiles as he led the young women from the room.

At the table, Joshua found himself next to Laurel. Her precious Jason was at the opposite end next to his sister. Joshua wondered who had made the seating arrangements.

Laurel's eyes dared him to say a word as he seated himself. He smiled; he was going to enjoy this.

Quiet conversations arose between partners as the meal was served. Since Laurel was seated by her father, whose attention rested on his wife, she was left to Joshua. He watched her squirm in discomfort. He knew she didn't want to speak with him, but neither did she want to be rude. He turned his most charming smile upon her.

"You look stunning this evening, Miss Marston."

Surprised at his compliment, Laurel looked up into his face. His gaze held hers and she found herself unable to do anything but stare at him.

"Have you found the time to enjoy another excursion into the swamp?"

That caught her attention. "Uh . . . no," she muttered, returning her eyes to her plate.

"That's a shame. I suppose you've been . . . otherwise occupied." Joshua glanced toward the other end of the table, catching Jason's stony look.

"Yes, I have."

"Will you be taking Jason into the swamp? To show him around your little piece of heaven?" He already knew the answer to that one. Laurel stared at him a moment, then at Jason. Jason would never go into her swamp. She hadn't even bothered asking him. Ignoring Joshua's question, she continued eating.

"I don't suppose you have to make a wager with him to receive compliments. My guess is that he knows how to pay a compliment to any woman, beautiful or otherwise." Joshua sneered down the table at the blonde peacock. He might have a problem with prim and proper ladies, but he realized that he was beginning to dislike pompous gentlemen even more.

Laurel's soup spoon froze in mid-air at his remark. *He's saying I'm ugly*, she gasped to herself. *I've never been so insulted in my life. I may not look like Marissa Ferguson, but I know I'm not ugly.* Carefully setting her spoon in her bowl, she turned glittering eyes to Joshua.

"At least Mr. Portland is a gentleman. He would never dream of telling a lady that she wasn't pretty." She refused to let him see the hurt his words had caused her.

Joshua persisted. "What about his kisses, Miss Marston?" he whispered. " Are they able to melt your frozen little heart?"

Laurel gasped out loud and everyone at the table turned to her. "Are you all right, Laurel?" Maida asked in concern, seeing the pallor of the younger woman's face.

"I'm fine, Maida." From the corner of her eye, Laurel could see Jason's frown. "I choked on my soup, but I'm fine now." With her reassurance, conversation returned to normal.

"It's amazing how easily that lie just rolled off your lips," Joshua taunted. "I wonder how many others you've told to become so good at it."

Laurel's cheeks burned with embarrassment and anger. She had told lies to her father, especially when it came to her swamp trips. But she would not be accused of deliberate and continued deception against her family. With an icy stare, she raised her voice.

"Mr. Douglas, would you be so kind as to escort me outside for a moment? I find I'm having difficulty catching my breath again."

Joshua's eyes narrowed, but he could do nothing but accept the invitation. *What is she up to*, he wondered. There was only one way to find out. Taking her hand, he led her onto the front porch and into the evening air.

The moment they were away from prying eyes, Laurel jerked her hand away. "Mr. Douglas, I don't know what I have done to deserve such rude and outrageous remarks, but I would appreciate it if you would desist."

Joshua chuckled mockingly, his eyes cold, hard gems of blue. "Or what? What are you going to do if I don't, Miss Marston? Have your gentleman friend defend your honor? I don't think so." Taking her by surprise, he lifted one of her clenched hands and eased it open, tracing her palm.

"To think these little hands could cause so much pain," he reminded her of her stinging slap in the swamp. "Maybe I should warn Mr. Portland before he becomes too attached to you. We men have to stick together against you ladies."

His finger continued almost unwillingly to brush her palm.

Laurel stood transfixed, the warmth of his touch sending goosebumps racing up her arm. She tried to tug it free and he strengthened his grip. His eyes darkened noticeably as he caught her gaze.

"I think we'd better go back in," she whispered hoarsely. Shaking his head, Joshua slowly pulled her closer.

"No man deserves the pain you women can cause. You rule us, you un-man us, and you never bat an eye." He drew Laurel against him. She couldn't breathe. His eyes were haunted.

"Do you deserve the love of a man, Laurel Marston? Will you protect his heart and keep it safe? Or will you tear it to shreds once he hands it to you?" Joshua lowered his head.

Laurel closed her eyes, anticipating the kiss she knew was coming. She should draw away—she knew she should—but she wasn't able. She wanted this kiss. She needed it.

Poised over her, Joshua halted. He stared down at her exquisite features. He hadn't expected this. True, he had goaded Laurel at the table and followed her outside fully intending to harass her. He had even decided just now that he would kiss her.

But he had not counted on the intensity of emotion she evoked in him. He felt that he was losing control, that he had already lost control. And that was something he had sworn would never happen to him again. He would not give in to his desire for this woman. He was afraid that, if he did, he'd never get out again.

Laurel's eyes flew open as Joshua jerked away. The look of disgust on his face was eloquence itself. With a cry, she fled from the porch.

Taylor sighed. It had been a long day. After the evening meal, she and Kendra had taken Joshua for what was ostensibly a stroll in the garden. Court had met them there with a trembling Lizy.

Taylor had been amazed at Joshua's calming effect on the young girl. With a gentle voice, he had reassured her of the overseer's dismissal, asked her forgiveness, and invited her to return to her family.

"I promised your family and the rest of the workers that I would treat you all with respect and that you need never fear me. May God witness my oath, Lizy," he had said. "Will you come back?"

Lizy was happy to agree, and Joshua had smuggled her into his wagon and taken her home. Taylor, Court, and Kendra were left to sigh in relief that the whole ordeal was over. It had been a nerve-wracking week.

Now Taylor sought out Maida in the parlor, hoping to have a moment alone with her sister-in-law.

"Maida, may I speak with you a moment?" Excusing herself, Maida followed Taylor out to a secluded corner of the veranda.

"What's the matter, Taylor?" she asked quickly.

Taylor took a deep breath. "I wanted to apologize for the way I've been behaving lately. I know you've been concerned and have wanted to help. But there was nothing you could have done."

"'Done'? I take it you've solved the problem?"

Taylor smiled. The afternoon with Ward had been wonderful. They had talked for hours—about their marriage, about children, even about Marissa Ferguson. Ward had reassured her on every topic.

"Yes," she said dreamily. "It's been solved."

"I'm glad to hear that, Taylor. You're the strong one in this family, and seeing you so upset has bothered me tremendously."

"Yes, well. The reason I wanted to apologize is because I've been jealous of you."

"Me? Whatever for?"

Taylor glanced down at Maida's stomach. "Because you're having a baby and I want to have one. I was feeling like a failure as a wife and I hated those emotions." It was so much easier to talk about now, she thought.

"I'm sorry, Taylor. I never realized." Maida hugged her friend. "We'll just have to start praying for God to give you a child too. If He could do it for Sarah and Abraham, why not for you and Ward?"

Laughing, they linked arms and returned to the parlor.

It was now the first of September, and the summer heat was giving way to the cooler temperatures of autumn. The Portlands had been visiting Catawba for several weeks. Laurel had enjoyed Jason's company, but she was ready for a change. When Pickle invited her to join him in the swamp, she accepted eagerly. They were there now, in their favorite clearing.

"Well, girl, you've had a few weeks with that dandy man. You still think he wants to marry you?" Pickle's dark eyes scanned the trees around him happily; he too was glad to be here. It would be one of the last times they'd have to get away to the swamp before winter.

Wrapping her arms around her knees, Laurel rested her chin on them and gazed down at her sturdy boots. "I'm quite certain he will ask for my hand."

"You don't look too happy."

"Oh, I'm happy." Laurel shrugged her shoulders. "I've known Jason Portland most of my life. He is a suitable match."

"But you don't love him," Pickle stated.

Laurel's head snapped up. "What difference does it make whether I love him or not? My father married Maida without love. I'll grow to care for him. He's a good man—kind-hearted and tender. That's what I want. Not a barbarian." She sighed crossly.

The chance to get away to the swamp today had been more than Laurel could resist. She had begged Kendra to make excuses for her absence. Kendra had reluctantly agreed and early this morning, Laurel had met Pickle outside, ready for an exciting day. Instead of having an enjoyable time, however, she was answering question after question about Jason.

"Now, girl, don't go gettin' upset with old Pickle. I just wants the best for you. If you think this English feller is it, then I'm happy."

Watching Pickle intently, Laurel decided that his words were sincere. Her eyes roamed over him, noting his black hair sprinkled with gray. The leathery skin of his face might hide the years, but they showed in his bent back. No one knew exactly how old he was. And Laurel couldn't imagine life without him.

"Please, Pickle, I don't want to talk about marriage or Jason or anyone else. I just want to enjoy our day."

"All right, Miss Laurel. Come on." Pickle rose. "Let's get on out and set our traps."

Eagerly, Laurel followed the old man. She wanted her mind off of Catawba. The past few weeks had been filled with Jason Portland and his compliments. Elated, Laurel had enjoyed each and every one. But lately, the words had seemed repetitive and empty. *Could a person get tired of compliments?* she wondered. Surely not.

To make matters worse, Joshua Douglas had been coming around more and more. He was there most evenings. If he wasn't spending time with Kendra, he was with Ward. Or Clair Portland. Clair absolutely glowed in the man's presence. To Laurel, it had been almost unbearable.

She had even contemplated speaking to Clair about her friend's actions around Joshua. But each time she'd started, her words sounded jealous. She certainly didn't want to give Clair the impression that she was interested in Joshua Douglas. So she kept silent.

Laurel had refused to speak a single word beyond polite greetings to Joshua. Sometimes she wondered if he enjoyed antagonizing her. He went out of his way to make mocking and sarcastic remarks, hiding behind an insincere smile and cold eyes. He was insufferable.

Laurel shook her head, clearing unpleasant thoughts. "I just want some peace," she muttered under her breath as she tramped after Pickle.

"What you say, Miss Laurel?" Pickle called over his shoulder.

"Nothing."

As Laurel's eyes followed Pickle's figure, an overpowering feeling of fear came over her. She tried to figure out what was causing it. Was it marriage? Certainly not. She'd been counting the days until she became a wife. Something else? She couldn't think of anything. Shrugging, she pushed aside the unsettling feeling and made an effort to enjoy the swamp life around her.

It wasn't until they sat down for their small noon meal that the feeling began to overwhelm her again. This time, Laurel tried to talk about it. "Pickle, have you ever done something that you knew was going to be the last time?"

"What you talkin' 'bout?"

"I'm not sure. I just have this feeling I won't be back in this swamp with you again." Biting into a slice of bread,

Laurel filled her mouth to keep the rest of her words from spilling out. Her thoughts were making her nervous.

"Well, maybe that be the way to know you be leavin' Catawba soon. If'n you marry that English man you sure to go to his home back in England." Pickle wiped his mouth with the back of his hand.

"England? I guess I never thought about that." Laurel had come to love Catawba and this harsh land. Leaving it would break her heart. Could she leave her family behind?

"You wantin' that man to ask you to marry him and you not thinkin' bout goin' back to his home?" Pickle snorted.

Laurel hadn't thought about much of anything lately. Her days had been filled with Jason Portland escorting her around the grounds, sitting and talking, reading aloud. Everything she did was with him. Little did he know, his company helped keep the hurtful things Joshua said from disturbing her too much. Joshua might not find her attractive, but Jason certainly did.

What would it be like to return to England and not see her family, Pickle, or the swamps? "Do you suppose he'd want to stay here?" she asked.

Pickle laughed. "Don't fret none, Miss Laurel. Wait 'til he asks you, then find out 'bout where you gonna live. If you loves him, you go where he goes."

"I suppose." Laurel muttered. *But to leave Catawba forever . . . ?*

Yates bent over the ledgers. He was amazed at how much money they'd made. Cotton, lumber, and horses were becoming more and more lucrative in the South and Catawba was profiting considerably. A knock on the door interrupted him.

"Am I disturbing you, Mr. Marston?" asked Jason Portland.

"Of course not, Jason. Come in." Yates motioned to a seat in front of his desk. "What can I do for you?"

Jason chose his words carefully. "I was wondering, sir, if I might speak to you about something important."

"Certainly." Yates knew the young man was here to ask for Laurel's hand in marriage. He had noticed how much time the two had spent together lately.

"You've known my family for many years, sir," Jason began. "We're a well-established old family. I wish to let you know that your daughter has come to mean everything to me." Taking a deep breath, he continued, "I believe Laurel would be a great asset to my family, and I would like to ask for her hand in marriage."

Yates looked intently at the young man. He was immaculately dressed, his blonde hair perfectly groomed. Nothing about him was out of order. Yates knew that Laurel wanted to marry Jason, but he hesitated. In business he had come to rely on his instincts. And they were telling him to turn the young man down.

He decided to take a chance. "As a father, Jason, I want the best for my daughters. I would like them to marry into good families, but I believe that it is more important that they be happy with their mates. I'm not going to give you my blessing until you ask Laurel herself."

"Excuse me, sir?" Jason was worried. His plan had not included this.

Holding up his hand, Yates tried to reassure him. "It's not that I disapprove. But I want Laurel to be the one to make the decision. If she agrees to marry you, then you have my blessing. But if she refuses, there is nothing I can do."

Jason hid a smile. He knew that Laurel would jump at the chance to marry him. Who wouldn't? She knew nothing of his financial difficulties. He was almost at the finish line.

"Thank you, sir. I appreciate your honesty and your love for your daughter."

"When do you plan to ask her?"

"I was hoping to do it soon. Possibly after dinner."

"Well, good luck to you, son. My daughter is a good girl, and she deserves all the happiness life can bring to her."

Seeing that he was dismissed, Jason stood, thanked Yates, and left. He was going to have to change his plans slightly. He hadn't counted on Yates Marston letting his daughter choose her husband. He was surprised—it was too much responsibility to give a female—but he figured that it was more of the Marston American barbarianism.

If he weren't careful, though, Laurel would end up choosing that American. Jason frowned. The man had been turning up at Catawba at the most inopportune times. When Jason and Laurel were in the parlor, he interrupted them. If they went strolling in the garden, he was there escorting one of the other Marston women. Wherever he and Laurel were, Joshua Douglas managed to be there too. It was getting so unbearable that Jason could barely keep from hiding his rage at the sight of his rival.

Clair wasn't any help, either. Jason had directed her to find out everything she could about the man, hoping to turn up some horrible secret from his past. But the twittering girl was so infatuated with Joshua, she did nothing but sing his praises.

According to her, the man could do no wrong.

The more he thought about it, the angrier he got. His sister and that American fool might ruin all his plans. He decided to pay a visit to Clair. It was time for her to pay for her inability to get information concerning Joshua Douglas. She hadn't taken his command seriously enough. Didn't she realize that their entire future lay in Laurel Marston's delicate hands?

Laurel trudged back into the yard at Catawba. Sweat trickled down between her shoulder blades. Her face was covered with dirt and her once-neat braid was in tangles. Pickle had already returned to do his chores, leaving Laurel to finish the last, short distance alone.

After Laurel refused to talk about Jason and marriage any further, she and Pickle had enjoyed the afternoon. Her premonition regarding the swamp still lingered, but she had refused to worry about it. If it was to be her last time in the swamp, Laurel wanted to enjoy every moment possible.

They had done some more trapping, and had found some unusual plants deeper in the swamp. But mostly they had talked. Laurel had been so content that she was reluctant to return to the plantation at the end of the day. Talking with Pickle was so different from talking with Jason. *Why is it so different?* she wondered.

She talked to Pickle about so many things. Things they both enjoyed. Pickle had wonderful stories to tell of his experiences in the swamps and woods of the South. She was fascinated with them and asked question after question.

But Jason liked to talk about different things. Apparently insignificant things. Every time that Laurel tried to bring up a more meaningful topic, such as the plantation or even politics, he patted her hand and told her not to worry herself. Laurel had gone along with it at first, but lately she had begun gritting her teeth to keep from saying something. Was that what marriage was going to be like with Jason? Would she only be allowed to speak of trivial and ladylike things?

The few times she and Joshua had talked had been much more stimulating. Would Joshua expect his wife to stick to fashion and the most popular furniture styles? She didn't think so. He would probably come home at night, weary from hard work, and share about his day—the good things and the bad. They would celebrate the good and solve the problems together. That's the kind of man Joshua Douglas was.

But he's not interested in me, she argued with herself. *He only seems to have eyes for Kendra and Clair. And what do I care?* Laurel hated to admit how jealous she was of the attention they received from Joshua. As much as the man was around, he never spoke with Laurel, except to trade insults.

Slipping into the house unobserved, Laurel swiftly made her way upstairs. There wasn't much time to get ready for dinner. She remembered, though, to thank Kendra for hiding her whereabouts from Jason. Kendra responded with a grimace and with a sigh, Laurel closeted herself in her room.

After a quick bath, Laurel carefully chose her garments, clothing herself in a pale blue gown. It was one of her favorites, with delicate white lace around the collar and sleeves. She knew that the pale color made her eyes look especially blue. Her hair she combed and piled atop her head in a braid. Putting on matching gloves and shoes, she went to the mirror. The calm, cool image before her in no way represented the tangle of feelings and thoughts hidden inside.

The family was already gathered in the parlor when she hurried in. Flushed from her efforts, she tried to compose herself before turning toward Jason. He would not approve of her dashing about, that was for certain.

"You look lovely this evening, Laurel," he complimented. *I've passed inspection*, she thought.

"Thank you, Jason." She glanced around the room, expecting to see Joshua. He wasn't there. In her disappointment, it took her a moment to realize that neither was Clair. She frowned.

"Where is Clair?"

"She is not feeling well. She asked me to make her apologies and hopes to see you tomorrow."

"Is there anything I can do?" Laurel asked, concerned for her friend.

Jason shook his head. "No. She'll be up and about tomorrow, I'm sure."

Laurel hadn't had much time with Clair. It seemed like every time they were alone, someone was interrupting them. Laurel felt bad. Clair had come all the way from England to visit her.

"Would you accompany me for a stroll, Laurel?" Jason asked, interrupting her thoughts.

"Shouldn't we wait until after supper?" Laurel didn't know why, but she didn't feel like being alone with Jason. After her afternoon's contemplation, she was finding it difficult to tolerate him.

"If that is your wish." Jason wasn't pleased with being put off, but there was nothing more he could say. He knew he should have waited until after dinner, but he had hoped to make their engagement announcement during the meal.

He wanted Laurel's acceptance as soon as possible. Enough time had been wasted on courting.

As soon as the meal was finished, Jason led her outside. A full moon cast Catawba into shadow. Stars glittered in the darkened sky. A whippoorwill called out its lonely whistle. Shivering slightly, Laurel wrapped her arms tightly around herself as Jason took her across the large porch.

"Did you enjoy your day, Laurel?"

Laurel knew Kendra had covered for her while she went to the swamp with Pickle. Yet there hadn't been time to ask her just what excuse she had made for Laurel's absence. Biting the inside of her lip, she hedged.

"Yes, it was nice. Thank you for asking." She was relieved when Jason simply smiled at her.

"I certainly missed you today. I've gotten quite used to your company." Jason drew Laurel to a bench.

Staring up at the sky, Laurel couldn't get over how black it was. For some reason, it reminded her of Joshua Douglas's hair. She had touched that hair. It had been surprisingly soft.

"Laurel?" Jason said impatiently. "Are you listening to me?"

Laurel quickly apologized for her rude behavior. Agitated at the direction her thoughts had taken her, she gave Jason her full attention. She refused to give another moment's thought to Joshua Douglas.

"What were you saying?"

Clearing his throat, Jason took Laurel's hand in his own. "I wanted you to know how I've come to feel toward you. You are everything that I could ever desire in a woman. You're beautiful, fashionable, and quite entertaining." He looked directly into her blue eyes.

"Laurel Marston, would you do me the honor of becoming my wife?"

Laurel gasped in surprise. "Wife? Me?" Dazed, she opened and closed her mouth. Why was her throat so tight?

"I know this is sudden, but I couldn't wait any longer. This morning I spoke with your father. He's agreed to accept whatever decision you make. What is your answer, Laurel?"

"I . . . I, uh, don't know what to say. I'm so shocked," Laurel stuttered. She couldn't believe her own reaction. She had hoped and prayed that Jason would ask her to marry him. But now that he was here waiting for an answer, she couldn't seem to get one out.

"Surely you guessed my intentions," Jason stated.

"Well, I had hoped, but I wasn't expecting it so soon." Laurel blushed and stood, putting a hand to her racing heart. She stepped to the railing and leaned against it. *This is what I've been waiting for*, she thought. *Why do I feel so numb?*

"Are you going to give me an answer, Laurel?" Jason persisted.

Laurel turned to stare at the Englishman. He looked pale in the moonlight. Pale? When Jason had first come to Catawba, she had thought him handsome. Why did he seem so pale now?

"I don't know what to say, Jason. Will you give me a little time to think about it?"

Pasting a smile on his handsome face, Jason acquiesced. "Anything you ask, dear lady. But please," he took her hand, "do not keep me waiting too long."

"I promise." The feel of Jason's mustache on her fingers made Laurel jittery. Pulling them quickly from his clasp, she hid them behind her back. All his pretty compliments and hand-kissing had excited her before. Why did it make her nervous now?

"Are you cold?" he asked, noticing her shiver.

"Just a little. Would you mind if we went back inside?"

"Not at all."

Returning to her family, Laurel saw the question in her father's eyes but, disconcerted by her indecisiveness, she averted her eyes. Moments later, pleading fatigue, she made her escape.

On the way to her room, Laurel knocked lightly on Clair's door. She didn't wait for a response, but entered quietly, easing the door closed behind her. Her friend was curled up under the bedcovers. A candle glowed on the nightstand, casting great shadows around the room.

"Clair?"

No answer.

Laurel tiptoed over to the bed and lightly shook Clair's shoulder. The girl yelped in pain and shot up in bed. Laurel jumped back in surprise.

"I'm sorry. I didn't mean to frighten you," she apologized. "I just wanted to talk to someone."

"Laurel?" Clair whispered. "What are you doing in here?" Pulling the blankets up to her chin, she propped herself against the pillows. A long-sleeved, high-necked gown of soft muslin covered her body.

"Are you feeling any better? Can I get you anything?" Laurel stepped around the bed. Hopping onto the empty side, she stretched out next to Clair. The two of them had spent many nights together just like this in England—sitting up together and talking about school and friends and whom they might marry someday.

"I'm fine."

"Are you too tired to talk?"

"No."

"Good." Enthusiastically, Laurel leaned over to hug her friend. Clair cried out. "Clair? What's wrong?"

"Nothing," Clair said quickly.

Laurel looked carefully at Clair's pale, shadowy face. Suddenly her eyes widened. She grabbed the candle and gasped in horror at what the light revealed.

"What happened to you?" Clair's cheek had a large, purple mark across it. Grabbing her arm, Laurel pushed up the sleeve of her gown. Ugly welts discolored her creamy skin.

"Clair!" gasped Laurel. Staring at the marks, she tried to figure out what could have possibly caused them. "Tell me what happened right now, Clair Portland."

"I fell down, Laurel. That's all." Tugging away, Clair tried to push her sleeve back down.

"Nobody could fall down and hurt herself this badly." She looked at her friend seriously. "Clair, we've been friends for a long time. Please tell me. Maybe I can help."

With a shaking moan, Clair broke down. Sobbing uncontrollably, she tried to tell Laurel what had happened. Laurel shook her head.

"Clair, I can't understand you. Who did this to you?"

Lips quivering, tears streaming down her face, Clair buried her face in the pillows. Laurel could only stroke her hair, trying to soothe her pain away. She waited patiently until Clair could speak. One word was all she said.

"Jason."

"What about Jason? Do you want me to get him?" Clair shook her head.

"He did this to me," she whispered.

Stunned, Laurel stared at the frail girl. The intensity in Clair's eyes told Laurel she had heard correctly. How could

Jason do such a thing to his own sister? Had Clair done something to displease him? Laurel couldn't think of anything that would warrant such a severe punishment. There had to be a reason, though. The Portlands weren't the type of people to hurt their own family. Were they?

"Why did Jason hit you, Clair?" Laurel asked.

Clair shivered, remembering.

She had been in her room, resting in the afternoon sunlight. The windows were open and she was reading a book. Jason had barged in without knocking. The fury on his face was the only warning Clair had before the first stinging slap.

"You've failed me again, Clair," Jason had whispered. That was the worst indication of his rage. Most people shouted when they were angry. Jason grew softer, more menacing.

"What have I done, Jason?" Clair had pleaded. Before the words were out, he struck again.

"Don't play dumb, Clair. It doesn't suit you. You've been out to destroy my plans since the beginning. You don't want me to marry Laurel. You don't want me to live in comfort. You want me to remain poor." Jason's rambling accusations had made no sense.

As if his own words spurred him on, Jason had ripped her book out of her hand and, throwing Clair to the floor, struck her over and over. Usually Jason's temper dissipated quickly. This time had been different. It wasn't until Clair had passed out from the pain that he had stopped.

Clair's eyes glazed over at the memory. Laurel was frightened. "But, Clair, you still haven't said *why* Jason did this to you." She couldn't help drawing back at the misery in Clair's eyes as her friend turned to her.

"I don't think I should tell," whispered Clair. "Jason wouldn't like it."

"Of course he wouldn't like it," flared Laurel.

"But, Laurel, I deserved it."

"What could you have possibly done to deserve this?"

Clair gingerly touched a bruise on her jaw. "It's been so pleasant being here at Catawba, Laurel. Jason has been so happy, he hasn't hurt me once."

"Until now," Laurel pointed out.

Clair closed her eyes. She could think of no reason not to tell Laurel now. "I made him angry," she whispered brokenly. "I always seem to make him angry."

"How often has this happened?" Laurel interrupted softly. She was afraid that if she spoke too loudly, Clair would stop.

"Oh, it's not very often." Clair's answer was horribly matter-of-fact.

"Is it once every few months?"

Clair twisted her fingers together in a knot, unable to meet Laurel's gaze. "It just depends. Sometimes he's fine for a few weeks, but other times he gets angry a lot—several times a week."

"He hits you several times a week?" Laurel asked in astonishment. "When did this start?"

"A couple of years ago. Shortly after you left to come here, I guess. Jason doesn't know I know this, but I heard him and Father arguing one evening because our finances have dwindled down to almost nothing."

Clair couldn't control her quavering voice. "It was late at night. I don't ever remember Jason being so angry. I should have gone back to my room, but I wanted to make sure he was all right. When he found me in the hall he lost control. . . . After it was over, he couldn't even remember lifting a hand against me."

Clair had avoided thinking about that evening ever since. It had been the beginning of the nightmare. Her maid had taken care of her, made her excuses, and kept prying eyes away. She had been in bed for several weeks recovering.

Laurel was sickened. "What made him angry this time?"

"You."

"Me?"

"Jason went to speak with your father about marriage. Instead of accepting Jason's proposal, he said you were to make the decision. He hadn't expected that. He's afraid that you'll choose Joshua Douglas."

"Joshua?"

"Mr. Douglas is a fine man," Clair whispered. "Gentle and caring. He would never hurt you, Laurel." She lay back in the bed and closed her eyes, worn beyond words.

Laurel stared at Clair. No, Joshua would never lift a hand to hurt her.

Torrents of rain beat against the windowpanes, almost masking the rumbles of thunder that echoed across the darkened sky. The wind was lashing through the trees. But inside the house, all was safe and secure. Candles flickered in the darkness, and a fire was lit in the parlor to keep out the chill. The men had gone to the office to wait out the storm while the women stayed in the parlor.

"How was Clair feeling this morning, Laurel?" Maida asked in concern.

"She was feeling better. I just hope she doesn't have a relapse. She was hoping to come down tomorrow." Laurel didn't like keeping things from the family, but she had promised to protect Clair.

"Have you made your decision about marrying Jason?" Kendra asked.

"How do you know about that?" Laurel demanded. It had only been two days since Jason proposed and she had spent most of that time with Clair. She didn't want to face Jason yet, so she'd pleaded headaches the last two days.

"Cammie told me," Kendra said, shrugging her shoulder.

Laurel sighed. Nothing happened on Catawba without Cammie's knowing it.

"Aunt Taylor," she said. "You've got to do something about Cammie's eavesdropping. I don't appreciate having my conversations repeated without my knowledge."

At that moment Cammie entered with a tray of tea and cakes. As she set it in front of Maida, she said, "If I don't listen, someone else will. Might as well be me. You gonna answer Miss Kendra's question?"

"I'm still thinking about it," Laurel mumbled.

"I thought you loved him," Maida said. "Why do you have to take so long with your answer? You should never keep a young man waiting too long. He may think you don't care for him."

Squirming nervously, Laurel tried to formulate a quick answer that would bring an end to the questions. "I'm just not sure about leaving Catawba. I've grown to love it here and would miss it terribly."

"So you're not concerned about leaving your family, just Catawba," Kendra joked.

Glancing up, Laurel looked at the women. "I would miss you all most of all," she whispered, unshed tears sparkling in her eyes.

"Well," Taylor said, patting Laurel's shoulder as she passed by to look out the window, "take your time. We want you to be happy, and if leaving here makes you unhappy, then we want you to stay."

Taking the opportunity to change the subject, Laurel laid her sewing aside and joined Taylor at the window.

"It certainly is black out there."

"Yes."

"I'm glad we're in here and not out there. This is a terrible storm!" Laurel shivered, thankful to be inside.

A banging on the front door made them jump. Taylor and Laurel looked at each other in surprise.

"I'll get it," said Laurel and went into the hall. As she opened the great oak door, the wind swept it from her grasp and smashed it against the wall. Her jaw dropped as she saw the bedraggled figure standing there.

"Marissa!"

Marissa Ferguson stood shivering in the doorway. Her teeth were chattering so hard she couldn't speak. Water dripped off of her to puddle on the floor. Laurel took control as all of Pickle's survival teachings came into play. Pulling her trembling friend into the parlor, she set her in front of the fireplace.

"Cammie, run upstairs and bring the quilts off my bed. And get one of my dresses for her to change into. Kendra, tell someone to get a room ready for her." Cammie and Kendra hurried out of the room. "Now, Marissa, lean closer to the fire. You're going to catch a chill. Maida, could you get her some hot tea?"

By the time Marissa had her tea in hand, Cammie had returned with a pile of quilts and one of Laurel's gowns. Together they helped Marissa undress. She shivered as she stood in her damp undergarments.

"Cammie, we need to rub her down." Laurel began a vigorous massaging of Marissa's arms. Up and down she rubbed, trying to get the blood flowing. As they repeated the ritual on her legs, Marissa started to smile. She enjoyed the attention.

"Are you feeling better, Marissa?"

A sigh of contentment whispered from Marissa's lips. "Yes, thank you, Laurel. You've saved me." She stretched gracefully, and Taylor, who had been watching the scene from a corner, narrowed her eyes.

"Then do you mind telling us what in the world you were doing out in that storm?" Laurel knew Marissa had her faults, but she certainly wasn't stupid.

"I was coming over to see your Uncle Ward," she slanted a look at Taylor, "and the first crack of thunder spooked my horse. The stupid beast reared, threw me to the ground, and ran off. I was closer to Catawba than my own home, so I came here." Marissa pouted prettily.

"You've been walking in this storm since it started?" Laurel asked in astonishment.

"Yes."

Laurel shook her head disbelievingly. Maida, eyebrows raised, left to see about some food. Taylor, who had Laurel's dress, wordlessly held it out, her face expressionless.

"Thank you, Aunt Taylor." Laurel helped Marissa put it on. It was a soft green muslin and it draped to the floor perfectly, the color enhancing her creamy complexion and auburn curls.

"I'll see if a room has been finished for you," said Laurel as she left the room.

"Would you like to lie down?" Taylor asked politely, indicating one of the sofas.

"No, I don't think so." Marissa walked to a mirror and checked her appearance, smoothing her hair. "Where are the men?" she asked casually.

"In the office."

"Oh. Would you mind getting Ward for me? I need to speak with him." Marissa continued her stroll around the room, dismissing Taylor.

"Actually, I do mind," Taylor said softly.

Stopping in her tracks, Marissa turned to eye the older woman. "Excuse me?"

"I said no," Taylor repeated firmly.

Marissa's brown eyes began to glitter dangerously. She stood directly in front of Taylor. "I think you'd better do as I ask, or you'll be sorry," she snapped.

This was too much for Taylor, who had fled England and a murderer rather than be forced into marriage, indentured herself when her money was stolen, and then married a man she hardly knew. She began to laugh. Collapsing into a chair, she laughed so hard that tears streamed down her face. If this spoiled little girl thought she could threaten Taylor Craven Marston, she was in for a big surprise. The idea brought on fresh gales of laughter.

Marissa stared at Taylor as if she'd lost her mind. Crossing her arms over her breasts, she announced. "This is not something to laugh about, Taylor. I meant what I said. If you're not going to get Ward for me, I'll find him myself."

Lifting the edge of her skirts, Marissa turned toward the door. Before she'd taken more than a few steps, however, she was jerked to a stop. Taylor had stepped on the hem of her gown. When Taylor spoke, her voice was soft but firm.

"I'm going to tell you this only once, Marissa Ferguson. Ward Marston is my husband, and he's going to remain my husband. Nothing you can do will change that. Do you understand me?"

Marissa was taken aback for a moment. Then a small smile began to lift the corners of her mouth. "Could it be that you're afraid Ward would leave you if the opportunity arose?"

"No," Taylor stated calmly.

Marissa sneered. "I wouldn't be so sure of that. You don't know what your husband does when he's with the horses all day. You're never there . . . but I am. I'm the one who shares his love of horses. I'm the one who spends time talking to him about his dream of becoming the best horse breeder around. I can share things with him." Jerking her dress from Taylor's grasp, she continued spitefully. "Perhaps you're no longer needed. Ward can come to me for the warmth and love he needs."

"Don't you think you should ask me what I need?" a deep voice asked from the doorway.

Both women whirled around. Marissa recovered quickly. "Ward, hello. I was just telling Taylor I needed to see you."

"So I heard," Ward commented dryly. "What are you doing out in this storm, Marissa?"

"Oh," she said shrugging. "I was on my way over and my horse threw me."

"Really? You're the best rider in the county and you let your horse throw you?" Ward raised his eyebrows. Stepping forward, he took Taylor by the hand and led her over to one of the sofas. But, instead of seating her next to him, Ward pulled her into his lap.

"Ward," Taylor gasped in humiliation. Pushing at his chest, she tried to break free of his hold.

"Be still, Taylor," he ordered firmly before glancing at Marissa. His face hardened. "I believe you need to hear something directly from me, Marissa. I love Taylor with all my heart. She is my wife and will remain my wife until death do us part. I will not allow this . . . misconception of yours to go any further. Am I understood?"

Marissa stood frozen for one instant while the color drained from her face. Then, "Very well," she spat and whirled from the room.

Taylor continued to struggle in Ward's arms. "Ward Marston, you are despicable. How could you make such a scene in front of that poor girl? And," she turned to look up at him, "how did you come to be standing in the doorway at that very moment?"

"Cammie," Ward answered blandly. His eyes twinkled at her.

"Oh, you. . . ." Taylor's smile was quickly covered by her husband's lips.

It wasn't until some time later that Ward reluctantly loosened his hold on her. "I suppose we should make sure she's taken care of. We don't want her coming down with a cold and having to stay here, do we?" He stood and set Taylor carefully on the sofa. "But I had better find you still here when I get back." With a look full of promise, Ward left the room.

Taylor snuggled back on the sofa and listened to the storm outside. The warmth of the fire was nothing compared to the warmth in her heart.

Court and Pickle sat together in their cabin, listening to the rain beat against the log roof. A sudden crack of thunder caused both of them to jump. Pickle went to the window.

"If'n that get any closer, we could fry some supper without makin' a fire." He peered out toward the barn.

Court chuckled wryly. "If that gets any closer, you're not going to find me taking the time to cook anything. I'll be hightailing it to the house." He watched the older man for a moment. "It's not going to do any good standing there. The horses will be fine."

Pickle turned around, shaking his head. "I don't know 'bout that. Those animals bound to get riled up. I know I shoulda stayed with 'em."

Court merely shrugged and went back to his work. He was whittling a piece of wood. He wasn't sure what he was making yet, but the repetitive movements helped keep his mind off of other things.

He sighed. He didn't know who he thought he was fooling. His mind was filled day and night with Kendra. His heart broke anew as he pictured her warm, dark hair and winsome smile. She was all he had ever wanted in a woman. Why in the world did she have to come from such a different way of life? Savagely he raked his knife across the wood.

Pickle silently watched him from across the room. He had watched Court all evening as he restlessly paced around the room. Now the older man spoke. "You gonna tell me what's botherin' you?"

Court looked up guiltily. "Nothing."

"Um-hmmm." Pickle looked at him significantly. Court stared at him a moment and he lifted an eyebrow. "You might as well tell me, boy. You been actin' like a caged animal for days."

Court finally gave up. He told Pickle everything. He told how he had first fallen in love with Kendra that day on the docks two years ago. He told of how horrible he'd felt when he realized that she was the daughter of his boss and how he had fought so desperately against his feelings. He told the older man about how Kendra had returned those feelings and how they had had two years of blissful, hidden romance. And then he told of how he had realized it wouldn't work—that he had broken it off with Kendra. Pickle sat there shaking his head in amazement. Court scowled at him.

"Well, now you know. Aren't you going to say anything? Something about how you can't believe how stupid I was to fall for the boss's daughter?"

"Yeah, I got something to say. I don' think I've ever seen anyone as foolish as you, boy. You're tearin' yourself apart over her and she's not much better. What you think you accomplishin' by this?"

Court glared at him angrily. "Don't even start with that, Pickle. I know what I'm doing. There's no way this thing could ever have worked out with me and Kendra, so I'm setting her free now while she has a chance to find someone else." He stood and walked to the window. "She can have someone like Joshua Douglas," he muttered. A flash of lightening lit his glowering face.

"Joshua Douglas?" Pickle said with a snort of laughter. "Joshua Douglas? Boy, you sure are a fool. Joshua Douglas no more got his mind on Missy Kendra than you got your mind on Missy Ferguson." He shook his head, chuckling. "No, siree. That boy got his eye on someone else entirely."

Court eyed him suspiciously. "What do you mean?"

"Why, he after Missy Laurel, and she done fallen head over heels in love with him too. 'Course, she don' quite know that yet, but she'll come 'round."

Court was dumbstruck. "Laurel? And Joshua? You're kidding."

"No, I'm not." Pickle nodded matter-of-factly. "You shoulda seen them two together in the swamp. The sparks was flyin', that's for sure." He came to stand beside the younger man, looking out at the storm-ridden night. "So don' you worry none 'bout Joshua Douglas. You hold on to Missy Kendra. She's a good girl."

Court fiddled with his whittling, thinking this new development over. He sighed and leaned against the windowframe. It really didn't change things anyway. He had made his decision and as much as it pained him, he would stick by it. Kendra would thank him someday. She didn't really realize yet that taking him meant giving up the beautiful house and the finery she was used to. She shouldn't have to do that.

Looking down, he saw that he had etched a "K" into the wood, and with an exclamation, he tossed it down. Pickle shook his head, turning back to the window just as a particularly savage crack of thunder shook the glass.

"That does it," he said, grabbing his coat from a nail by the door. "I know those horses be scared out their mind. I goin' over to check on them."

"I don't know, Pickle. Perhaps you should wait," Court started, but Pickle was shaking his head.

"I know what I'm doin'. Don' worry, I won' be long." With a smile, he went out the door. Looking out the window, Court could see the old man running through the rain toward the barn. With a sigh, he turned and went back to his whittling.

Taylor again curled against her husband. After seeing that someone took Marissa to her room, Ward had returned as promised to the parlor. She had been waiting for him, and they had spent a lovely half-hour in front of the fire.

"Do you know how much I love you?" Ward whispered now as he pulled her close. She went willingly into his arms.

The sound of the front door banging open drove them apart. Leaping to his feet, Ward was in the hall before Taylor could gather up her skirts. She followed to find

Court standing there soaking wet. The two men were talking so rapidly she couldn't follow the conversation.

"What's happened, Court?" She asked.

"There's been an accident."

"Who?"

"Pickle." Court ran a shaking hand through dripping red hair.

"I'll come right away. Maybe Laurel should come too." Taylor turned to run upstairs for her niece. Ward reached out a hand to restrain her.

"Taylor, it's too late. Pickle's dead."

"Dead?" she repeated woodenly. Her eyes darted from one man to the other. It couldn't be true, she thought in confusion. Not Pickle. He was part of their family. "What happened?"

Before Court could explain, Laurel came down the stairs. "I heard the door." She stopped short when she saw the look on Court's face. "What's wrong?"

"Let's go into the parlor," Taylor suggested, taking Laurel by the arm. "Court, come warm yourself by the fire. You can tell us everything."

"What's going on, Aunt Taylor?" Nervousness made Laurel's voice shrill.

Taylor led Laurel to the sofa she had just vacated. Seated beside her, she tried to break the news gently. "Laurel, there was an accident." Choking momentarily on the rush of tears, she paused to pull herself together. "Pickle is dead, honey."

Staring first at her aunt's stricken face then at the two men, Laurel went white. "Pickle? Dead?"

"Court, tell us what happened," Ward prodded.

Curling the brim of his hat, Court tried to put everything together in his own mind.

"We were settling the horses down this afternoon before the storm. Some of them were acting crazy—kicking the walls and rearing up in their stalls. Pickle didn't want to leave them, but I made him come back to the cabin. I knew there wasn't anything he could do.

"As the storm grew worse, though, Pickle insisted on checking on the horses. I couldn't persuade him to wait, so he went out. When he didn't return after a while, I decided to check on him." Court paused and took a breath.

"When I got to the barn, the horses were out of control. The lightning and thunder were cracking so loudly and frequently that they couldn't calm down. I called out to Pickle when I got inside, but he didn't answer."

Court's voice broke. "I found him in the last stall with the new stallion. He'd been trampled," he whispered.

A cry was wrenched from Laurel. Burying her face in her hands, she wept for her friend. *How can I go back to the swamp?* she thought. *It will never be the same without Pickle.*

Her sobs echoed throughout the house, bringing the remainder of the family into the parlor. She refused to be comforted, though, and was finally carried upstairs by Yates. The rest of Catawba was silent.

Far away, under a gentler sky, Treet lay on his back looking up at the stars. The wind was pushing clouds across the sky; there would be rain soon.

He looked over at Reid. The boy was fast asleep, tangled up in his blanket. Treet smiled. The young master had been having a grand time on this trip. He had chattered non-stop all the way to Virginia, and was proceeding to chatter all the way back. He had done a good job, though, Treet had to admit. He had handled himself like a man during the sale of the stallion. The buyer had been inclined to haggle, but one look at Reid's determined face and he had backed down. Reid had puffed out his chest and solemnly shaken the buyer's hand just as he'd seen his Uncle Ward do.

Of course, as soon as the man had left, Reid had let out a whoop that startled everyone around. But he had quickly pulled himself together and had acted the young gentleman the rest of the day. The two of them had enjoyed the city accommodations that night, getting a good meal and a bath before heading out on the return trip. They would both be glad to get home.

Treet sighed, his thoughts turning, as they seemed to do with increasing regularity, to Cammie. He pictured her snapping brown eyes and broad smile and the feel of her body as she had said goodbye to him the day they left. Try as he might, he could not make himself forget her as he'd sworn he was going to do. With each passing day, he realized how much he missed her. He even missed little Daniel.

With a groan, Treet rolled over. He might as well admit it to himself now and get it over with. He was in love with Cammie, and that's all there was to it. He smiled to himself as he realized what he'd done.

"I'm in love with her. I'm in love with my Cammie girl, and I believe I want to marry her."

He couldn't keep from grinning at the release of pressure he'd built up on the trip. Rolling back over, he stared up at the heavens. Since his wife and sons had been taken from him, he had steadfastly refused to love or be loved. He hadn't thought about God either. His wife had been a God-fearing woman, but Treet had blamed him for his loss.

Now, he thought of Cammie and what he could be losing again.

"God," he whispered, "if you there and you listening, thank you for sending me Cammie and little Daniel." He took a deep breath. "And thank you for showing me before it was too late. Amen."

Across the fire, on his own bedroll, Reid smiled to himself and went back to sleep.

As the sun peeked over the horizon, Laurel wiped away the last of her tears. She had mourned for Pickle all night. Now was the time for action. Reaching into the wardrobe, she pulled out her swamp outfit for the last time.

After changing, she jotted a short note to her family and propped it on her pillow. They wouldn't be able to find her even if they wanted to. She quietly slipped from the room.

Kendra listened to the family bombard Court with questions. She wanted to tell everyone to leave him alone. Fatigue was etched in every line of his face. She fought her sudden desire to hold and comfort him.

At that moment, Court glanced toward Kendra. He froze. Everything she felt shone in her dark eyes. He tore his gaze away and refused to look at her again.

There hadn't been many questions last night, but Ward had asked him to come to the house first thing this morning. Laurel wasn't downstairs yet, and Court was relieved. The sound of her sobs had haunted his dreams all night.

"How is Miss Laurel this morning?"

"We haven't heard a thing from her yet. We didn't want to disturb her." Taylor had also heard Laurel's tears throughout the night.

"Couldn't disturb her even if'n you wanted to," remarked Cammie bluntly.

"What do you mean?" asked Taylor.

"She's gone. Up 'n' left this mornin' real early. I saw her."

"Where did she go?" Taylor persisted.

"Swamp."

"The swamp?" Yates exclaimed. "How do you know she went there?"

"She was dressed for it. That's where she goes when she's upset, and I'd say she's plenty upset today." Cammie continued picking up teacups as she talked.

"Do you think that's safe?" Maida looked worried.

"She be fine. That girl know everything 'bout the swamp that Pickle knew. Don't you worry none, Miss Maida."

"Maybe I should go after her?" Jason Portland asked. He'd remained a quiet bystander throughout the whole event. It was beyond his understanding why Laurel was so upset over a slave's death, but if it gave him a chance to soothe her he would take advantage of it. She still hadn't given him an answer to his proposal, and with each delay, Jason grew more nervous.

Kendra snorted. "You'd get lost before you set foot into the forest," she said rudely.

A slight flush stained Jason's cheeks. "I think we should go after her. She's so upset that she may get hurt."

"Excuse me," Court interrupted. Everyone looked at him. "There's only one person that would even have an idea of where to find her."

"Who?" everyone asked in unison.

"Joshua Douglas. He went out with Miss Laurel and Pickle one day, and he used to be a tracker."

"Then get him," Maida stated flatly. "I don't want Laurel out there alone."

Court raced over the soggy ground as quickly as he dared. The roads were so washed out that travel was difficult, but he was determined to reach Douglas's farm. Laurel's life could depend on it.

It wasn't easy to turn to the man whom he had thought loved Kendra. But at least he knew now it wasn't so. He was glad Pickle had straightened him out before he'd died. Just in case, though, Court hoped to help the relationship along by sending Douglas after Laurel. Not that it mattered now, he told himself. He had to keep reminding himself of that fact.

Leaping from his saddle, he ran across the yard to Joshua's farmhouse and banged on the door. An older black man answered.

"I need to speak with Master Douglas."

"Yes, sir. This way." Court followed the man inside. Joshua's dark head was bent over a desk. "Someone to see you, sir."

"Thank you, Matthew." Glancing up, Joshua frowned, trying to remember where he'd seen the man before him. "Do I know you?"

"I'm Court Yardley from Catawba. I've come to ask for your help."

"Is something wrong?"

"It's Miss Laurel. She's gone into the swamp, and her family is worried about her. Her friend Pickle was killed yesterday and she took it hard. This morning she left for the swamp without telling anyone."

"Dear God," prayed Joshua. He came around the desk, bellowing toward the door. "Matthew!"

Instantly the door opened, and the man who had ushered Court in stood there. "I'll see your horse is readied and your clothes laid out," he said.

"Good." Joshua turned back to Court. "I'll be with you in a moment." Taking the stairs two at a time, he tore his clothes off and reached for the heavier ones Matthew was laying out.

"You're in love with this Miss Laurel, ain't ya, boy?" Matthew's gruff voice asked. Joshua didn't respond. "No use you ignoring me. I can see it in your eyes."

"You're seeing things, old man," Joshua countered.

"I think you better take a good look at your heart, boy. That girl means more to you than your own life and you know it." Matthew left the room.

Joshua stared after him. *What does he know, anyway?* he told himself. *Laurel Marston means nothing to me. She's going to marry that dandy Englishman and leave America for good. I'm just helping my neighbors by fetching her home safely. That's all.*

He almost believed himself.

Laurel's quick pace carried her through the fields and into the forest. Throughout the morning she continued walking through the dense bushes and trees. It was just before noon when she reached her destination. In the middle of their small clearing, surrounded by trees and brush, Laurel sat down.

This had been her and Pickle's favorite place. They had cleared it together. Crossing her legs, she allowed herself to remember all the times they'd had together. Pickle had been her friend. No one knew her the way he did. Quietly, she began to cry.

"Is there room for one more here?"

Laurel jumped and spun around. Who had found her here? As her tear-filled eyes focused on the man standing before her, Laurel realized it was the one person she wanted to be with.

"Joshua," she cried.

Not pausing to consider her actions, Laurel launched herself across the distance that separated them and into his arms.

This was where she wanted to be forever.

How did you find me?" Laurel whispered.

"Court came for me. Your family was worried about you."

Joshua couldn't breathe for a moment as he felt her small body against his. Laurel pulled back, but not far enough to loosen his hold.

"But how did you get here so fast? I left early this morning and I just now got here."

"I rode my horse. I was able to make it quite a ways before abandoning him," Joshua explained.

"You know about Pickle," Laurel choked out.

"Yes." Gathering Laurel close again, Joshua let her cling to him as fresh tears rolled down her cheeks and wet his shirt.

"Sssh. It's going to be all right, sweetheart. You'll see."

"Oh, Joshua, I can't stand it. I've lost my friend and now I have no one."

Joshua shook his head. "What about your family?"

"I don't mean them. I mean someone who is all mine. Pickle and I were best friends. Sometimes he knew my very thoughts. I could be myself with him and not worry about being judged."

Joshua took her hand and seated her on a nearby log. Straddling it, he faced her. "Laurel, you can be yourself around your family. They love you."

"You don't understand, Joshua. My family expects me to act like a proper lady. That's fine sometimes—during parties or around guests—but on my own I want to go hunting or hiking around through the swamp. My family would never understand that."

Joshua reached out to wipe a tear from her cheek. "Why don't you give them a chance? I'm sure Kendra would like a sister like you just described to me."

Laurel jerked back and glared at him. "You seem to be very close to my sister. All the time you've spent with her makes you an expert, I suppose."

Joshua's mouth twitched. "Are you jealous?"

"Jealous! Of you and Kendra? Never," Laurel huffed. Standing, she started to leave the clearing.

"Where are you going?" Joshua asked, following her.

"Home. I wouldn't want my family to worry any longer about me."

Joshua pulled her to an abrupt halt and glared down at her. "You're not going anywhere, yet. We're going to settle this once and for all."

Laurel made no move. Joshua sighed and ran a hand through his hair.

"Your sister is a sweet girl. She's enjoyable company and very informative when it comes to horses. That's why I spent so much time with her. That's all."

"You're not in love with her?" Laurel asked cautiously.

"Good Lord, no."

"Oh."

"Is that all you have to say?" For some reason that made him angry. "I have stood by and watched while that peacock Portland fawned all over you for several weeks now. I want to know where you stand with him. Are you in love with him?"

Laurel stared wide-eyed, shaking her head.

"Are you going to marry him?"

Again she shook her head.

"Will you marry me?"

Laurel started to shake her head again before Joshua's words sank in. Her mouth fell open. Had he really asked her to marry him? His proposal had been spoken so harshly she almost hadn't heard. "Marry you?" she squeaked. He continued glaring at her.

"Marry you?" Laurel was stunned into silence. The words that she had longed to hear filled her with joy. She wanted to scream "Yes!" at the top of her lungs. But she suddenly remembered, she had not given Jason Portland her answer yet.

Laurel took a deep, calming breath. *It wouldn't be right to give Joshua my answer before letting Jason know that I am refusing him,* she decided. But she couldn't tell Jason the answer without fear of his harming Clair again. She frowned as she tried to find a solution. Seeing it, Joshua's heart sank.

"Don't bother speaking, Miss Marston. I believe your inability to answer is clear enough." Turning on his heel, he began walking away.

"Joshua," Laurel pleaded, racing after him. She threw her arms around his neck, trying to stop him. "Please listen to me. Please," she begged.

Tugging her arms away, Joshua stood rigidly where she had caught him, not even looking at her.

"I want to give you an answer. But it's not that simple." Bowing her head, Laurel prayed that Joshua would understand. "Jason Portland has asked me to marry him, but I haven't given him an answer. I can't answer you until I've given him an answer." That was the closest Laurel could come to saying yes without actually saying it.

"Why didn't you tell your dandy Englishman you'd marry him?" Joshua asked fiercely.

"Because I found I no longer loved him."

"Is your affection so fickle, Laurel?"

"No. It just took me a while to find out what I really wanted. And since it was right before my eyes, always taunting me and ranting at me, it was difficult to recognize."

Her answer confused him. He turned. "What are you saying, Laurel?"

"I'm not saying anything definite until I've spoken with Jason, but I can tell you I love you."

Joshua stopped breathing. Laurel watched understanding wash across his face. Then, breaking into a huge grin, he snatched her up in his arms and twirled her around the clearing. She could only cling to him as, with a whoop of laughter, he stopped and rained kisses all over her face.

"You're mine, Laurel Marston. I've waited for a long time for just the right woman, and now that I've found her I'll never let her go." Tenderly cupping her face in his hands, Joshua looked into her eyes. "I love you."

"I love you, Joshua."

Slowly Joshua lowered his head, claiming Laurel's lips in a kiss that sent warmth to her toes. With a deep sigh of contentment she flung her arms around his neck, returning the kiss with every bit of love she had.

Moments later, gasping for air, they looked at each other in astonishment. "I've said it before, Miss Marston, and I'll say it again. You're definitely no proper lady."

"Are you insulting me, Joshua Douglas?"

"Insulting you! Sweetheart, to me a lady is a woman who only knows how to sew, supervise a household, and look pretty. That's what I thought you were the first evening we met. After closer inspection, I found there was more to you than first expected. And I'm glad I searched below the surface because I've found myself a gem I plan to cherish forever."

Snuggling back in his embrace, Laurel smiled. "Joshua, when did you know you loved me?"

He chuckled. "When we were here in the swamp the first time. The companionship you shared with Pickle made me jealous. You coped with everything and didn't bat an eye at the bugs or possible dangers. And then you showed me up in our trapping contest. That's the woman I fell in love with." He stroked her hair back from her face, marveling at its beauty. "What about you?"

"I think I knew the moment I saw you at the party. But you kept ignoring me. No one had ever ignored me that way, and it made me angry. It took me a little while to figure it out, but when Jason asked me to marry him, I knew I couldn't do it because I loved you."

"I'm glad you weren't foolish enough to accept that buffoon's proposal."

"Me too," Laurel said emphatically. The thought of Jason made her shiver. He was a cruel man. Turning him down was not going to be easy, and she wasn't looking forward to the confrontation. She wished that she could run home and tell everyone that she loved Joshua.

But first things first. Laurel would find Jason and break the news to him gently. She prayed he would accept the loss and not harm Clair. Now that she knew about his temper, Laurel was determined to see her friend protected.

Pickle would be happy for me, Laurel thought. *Marrying Joshua was all he wanted for me . . . and all I want.*

Seeing the mist of tears forming, Joshua pulled Laurel closer. "What's wrong, sweetheart? Are you missing Pickle again?"

Laurel shook her head. "I'm just thinking of how excited he would be knowing I was marrying such a fine man. He always thought you were the best match for me." They were quiet as they remembered their friend and each silently thanked him and God for bringing them together.

With Laurel snuggled closely in his arms, Joshua nudged his horse toward Catawba. It had been glorious sharing those few moments of solitude back in the clearing. He couldn't have asked for a more beautiful, passionate woman than his Laurel. She was so full of love that Joshua felt almost overwhelmed. How could someone so lovely and courageous be in love with him? He had always wanted a wife that could stand by his side in all circumstances. And that was exactly what God had blessed him with.

Thank you, Father, for giving me the desire of my heart, he prayed. *I will treasure Laurel and treat her with respect and love. Show me how to be the best husband I can to her. She is everything I could ever have hoped for. Thank you.*

Joshua chuckled softly, not wanting to disturb Laurel's sleep. Matthew had been right all along. That old man heard and saw more than was good for him. Joshua hoped that Laurel and his friend would get along together. Matthew was as important to him as Pickle had been to Laurel.

Joshua knew he would have to include Laurel in on his and Matthew's secret as well. He wondered how she would react upon finding that Matthew was a full partner at the farm. A black man wasn't allowed to own land, but Matthew received as much profit as Joshua did. Matthew pretended to be Joshua's personal servant, but the truth was that they were partners. Knowing how close she had been to Pickle, Joshua was sure that Laurel would understand. Especially sure, after finding out that Kendra and Taylor helped runaway slaves. The women of Catawba were headstrong and proud.

Smiling down at Laurel's sleeping head, he thought about the life they would make for each other . . . the children they would have, the things they would accomplish together. He was still smiling as his horse carried him into the yard at Catawba. The Marstons streamed from the house as Joshua reined to a halt.

"Laurel, we're home," he whispered softly, thrilled at the thought of her waking in his arms. Blinking her eyes sleepily, she looked into his deep, blue eyes.

"It wasn't a dream. You *do* love me," she murmured in awe.

"Yes, my love." He grinned down at her wickedly. "Now wipe that hungry look off your face. Your family is coming to greet us." In the blink of an eye, Laurel assumed a proper demeanor as Yates arrived to take her from his arms.

"Laurel Marston, I ought to beat you for scaring us like that. I don't ever want to hear of you going into that swamp alone again. Do you understand me, young lady?" Yates's scolding lost its sting as he crushed his daughter in his arms.

"I'm sorry, Father. I just had to go back one more time. I was fine, honestly." Laurel blinked back tears as she was hugged by the rest of the family. It was good to know that there were people who loved her like this. It wasn't until she was back in Yates's arms that he noticed her clothes.

"What on earth are you wearing?" he exclaimed, holding her at arm's length. Laurel had completely forgotten her swamp outfit. She was silent with embarrassment.

Kendra, on the other hand, was impressed with Laurel's invention. "I think it's great. Are you able to get around the woods easier?" Laurel only nodded, watching her father's expression. She was relieved when he only shook his head in mock amazement. There would be no lecture.

By this time, Joshua had climbed from his horse and was standing behind her. His nearness made her nervous. She didn't want Jason to get suspicious before she could speak with him. She was afraid he would take it out on Clair. She stepped away just as the front door flew open and Marissa Ferguson came flying down the steps.

"Joshua," Marissa cried, throwing her arms around his neck and planting a kiss on his lips. "Are you all right? I was so worried about you."

Mouth hanging open, Laurel watched the scene before her without moving. Then, eyes glittering angrily, she began advancing toward Marissa. Joshua quickly tugged the other woman's arms from around his neck and set her aside.

"Ah, if you ladies would excuse me, I must return to my farm. I have yet to see what damage was done by the storm."

With a wave to the family, he pulled himself back into his saddle and retreated, knowing he was a coward for taking off so abruptly, but also knowing he wasn't in the mood for Marissa's machinations. The family stood nonplussed at his hasty departure. It was Taylor who, with a sharp look at Laurel's face, suddenly understood and herded everyone back into the house, leaving the two girls alone.

"Marissa, would you help me upstairs?" Laurel's voice was sweetness itself.

"Certainly, Laurel. What are friends for?" With a last look at Joshua's retreating form, Marissa followed Laurel into the house. She was thoughtful as they went up the stairs. She didn't like being turned down by Ward Marston—it had been humiliating—but at least she still had Joshua Douglas. And he wasn't married. She would just have to turn her attentions to him. She smiled as she followed Laurel to her room.

Laurel's face was expressionless as she shut the door. "How are you feeling today, Marissa?" she asked, peeling off her swamp outfit. "Are you recovered from last night's ordeal?"

"Oh, yes. I'm feeling much better after having seen my Joshua."

"*Your* Joshua?" Laurel halted. "Aren't you assuming a little much?"

"I don't think so." Marissa went to Laurel's mirror and began preening. "Don't you remember—he kissed me."

"You're the one who told me that kissing other men didn't mean anything. Besides, how do you know Joshua Douglas isn't already spoken for?" Laurel was having a difficult time keeping her patience. Marissa had lied about her Uncle Ward, which was unforgivable. But having witnessed that scene with Joshua made her furious at her so-called friend.

Waving a hand, Marissa dismissed Laurel's comment. "With Joshua it means something. He makes me feel so alive when we kiss." She threw herself across Laurel's bed and smiled sensuously.

"Does that mean you've kissed him more than once?" Laurel pulled on a clean dress, amazed at how smoothly her questions were coming. She wanted to smack the other girl for speaking so about Joshua.

"Well, of course." Marissa smiled. "A number of times. He's been to my house for dinner on several occasions."

"Oh? When?"

Marissa finally noticed her friend's fierce look. "What's the matter with you, Laurel? Why are you looking at me like that?"

Laurel had had enough. Crossing to the bed, she glared down at the other girl. "Because I want you to know that Joshua Douglas belongs to me. He and I are in love, and you're going to keep your hands off of him from now on. No more throwing your arms around him, or kissing him, or even dancing with him." Laurel stood over Marissa, determined to make herself clear. Marissa laughed.

"Laurel Marston, you couldn't even begin to handle a man like Joshua Douglas. He's much too strong for you. Leave him to me. I'll take good care of him."

"No."

"No?" Marissa's brow raised.

"I said no, Marissa. And you had better believe I mean it. Don't lay another hand on him again, do you hear me?"

Laurel's softly-spoken words finally reached Marissa. She sat up and looked closely at her friend. Determination was written in every bone of Laurel's body. Her eyes glittered coldly as she stood prepared to defend her love and against her will, Marissa drew back from the expression on the other girl's face.

She really meant it, Marissa decided in surprise. *Just like Taylor, she really meant it.* Would there never be an end to the women of Catawba and the men they loved? With a sudden sneer, she pushed herself off of the bed and straightened her gown.

"Very well, Laurel, if that's the way you feel." She marched to the door. "I'll be leaving now. Don't expect to see me around here for a very long time." With a last haughty glance, the redhead slammed the door behind her.

Laurel sighed. Now that it was over, she felt almost sorry for Marissa Ferguson. It was obvious that the girl was on a self-destructive path. She would never find any happiness in life if she continued to have such misconceptions about love. Laurel sincerely hoped that Marissa would someday find someone who cared about her as much as Joshua cared about Laurel.

Now, though, Laurel had to deal with Jason. She was nervous—frightened even—of how he would react to her decision. But at least she had a small reprieve.

First they had to lay Pickle to rest.

A somber group stood over the mound of dirt as Ward Marston said a few words about Pickle. About what a good man he was and how loyal he had been. About how they would miss him. They were burying the body of a dear friend, but they knew the real Pickle was now in heaven. Laurel stood beside Kendra with dry eyes. She had said her goodbyes yesterday in the swamp. Pickle was in a much better place than Catawba . . . but she would still miss him dearly.

Afterward, as the family made their way back to the house, Musket began barking. Everyone turned to see a wagon trundling up the road. It was Reid, waving his hand frantically while Treet sat stoically beside him. Calling out their welcome, the family ran to greet them.

"Reid, you're back sooner than we expected," Ward said, clapping his nephew on the back as Reid came toward him. Reid smiled. There was something indefinably different about him. He seemed older. Covered with the grime and dust of the road, clothes askew, he had an air of confidence that hinted at changes in the boy that he was and the man he would become. The trip had been good for him.

"Treet and I were tired of being away from home. We've been traveling long and fast to get back." Finally noting everyone's somber attire, he asked, "What's going on?"

Laurel answered. "Pickle is dead, Reid. He died a few days ago."

"Oh, no! I'm sorry that I wasn't here. Pickle was a good man. He taught me all about horses." He faltered slightly, trying to act manly. "I'll miss him."

"Today is a day of joy, Reid," Ward said. "Pickle was lucky enough to get to heaven before any of us. So today we celebrate. Pickle would have liked that."

The gathering moved toward the house, missing one beloved man and rejoicing in the return of another.

Cammie ran to the barn as fast as her legs would carry her. Seeing Master Reid walk into the house with the family meant that Treet was home too.

"Treet," she called as she came in sight of him.

Treet turned with a huge smile and opened his arms as Cammie ran into them. Swinging her into the air, he laughed. "I missed you, Cammie girl."

"I missed you too, Treet."

He set her back on the ground, reluctantly releasing his hold on her. It felt so good to have her in his arms.

"How was the trip?" Cammie asked.

"Long and lonely," he answered. "Cammie, I've had the past several weeks to think about you. I did little else in my spare time. You were in my dreams every night.

"I have something to tell you. I've loved you for a long time, but I wouldn't admit it to myself. The pain of losing my wife and boys was more than I could bear. But I realized something. Even worse than losing someone is loving someone and not sharing your life with her because of fear. I can't live without you, Cammie girl, and I would be honored if you would marry me."

Squealing in delight, Cammie threw her arms around Treet's neck. He laughed again. "I take it that means yes?"

"Yes, yes, yes!" With each word she kissed his face.

"Good," he answered, suddenly serious. "Good."

The barn area was silent as they sealed their love for each other with a long, lingering kiss.

Laurel clasped her fidgety fingers behind her back. She had asked Jason to accompany her onto the porch. The rest of the family was busy filling Reid in on everything that had happened while he was gone.

"You wished to speak with me, Laurel?" Jason asked.

"Yes, Jason." Laurel tried to smile. Inside, she felt cold.

"I, uh, wanted to talk to you, Jason, about your proposal. I've thought about it a great deal. I want to say that I am truly flattered by your attentions. But I must decline your generous offer."

There, she'd said it. Laurel wanted to heave a great sigh of relief, but she knew that wouldn't be appreciated by Jason. Nervously, her eyes flitted to his face. It was white with shock.

"You're turning me down?" he whispered hoarsely.

Laurel jerkily nodded her head, attempting to keep her smile in place.

"I see. If you don't mind my asking—why?"

"Because I don't love you," she blurted.

Jason's face twitched, darkening with rage. Laurel's eyes widened at the transformation. She realized now why Clair was so afraid of him.

Jason sneered at her expression. "Yes, Laurel, you should be afraid," he whispered. "I don't think you understand the situation. You see, you have no choice. We *will* be wed before leaving for England next month. My family and livelihood depend on it. To be blunt, I need your money." He leaned closer. "Do I make myself clear?"

Laurel stood. She would not let this man dominate her as he did Clair. Using every bit of courage she could muster, she challenged him.

"Jason Portland, I have declined your proposal of marriage as politely as I could. There is nothing you can say or do to make me change my mind." She started walking away.

With a snarl, Jason grabbed Laurel's arm, whirling her around. "I am not finished with you. No woman turns her back on me. I won't have it. You will submit to me, Laurel, or you'll regret it. Like Clair." He laughed at the horror in her eyes. "Yes, Laurel, I know you found out about my . . . little flaw. Understand this—if you turn me down, I'll make sure you experience it firsthand."

Angered beyond reason, Jason slapped her, a stinging blow across her face. The sound echoed between them. Turning white, she struggled to pull free of his grip.

"Are you going to marry me, Laurel?" Jason asked.

"Never!" Laurel prayed that her family would hear them, but she knew that they were all the in the parlor talking and laughing.

"Ahh, a tough lady. It will give me great pleasure to make you submit." Without warning, Jason released her arm and pounded his fist into her belly. Laurel fell to her knees. Gasping for breath, she tried to regain her balance. Before she could move, though, he jerked her head up by the hair and slapped her again.

With a groan, she collapsed in a heap. A loud ringing filled her ears. She couldn't make sense of the noises she was hearing. Before Jason could deliver another blow, she sank into a welcoming blackness.

From a distance, Joshua saw Laurel on the front porch. With a smile, he hurried his horse forward. Then he noticed someone was with her. Jason Portland. In the instant that fact registered, he saw the Englishman strike her.

Without thought, he was out of the saddle and running toward the house. Growling deep in his throat, he leaped up the steps and snatched Jason by the collar just as Laurel sank to the floor unconscious. Over and over Joshua pounded his fists into the other man. It didn't matter that Jason wasn't protesting; Joshua's anger was so intense that he couldn't control himself. It wasn't until Jason's body slumped against him that Joshua tossed him aside and bent over Laurel.

"Laurel," he called softly, gathering her into his arms. "Honey, open your eyes."

Laurel didn't want to obey the voice that called to her through her cloud of pain. It persisted, though, and she slowly lifted her lashes.

"That's my girl," Joshua said. "I'm going to lift you now. It may hurt a little, but I have to get you inside. All right?"

Laurel nodded her head slightly. She just wanted to go back to sleep and not wake up until the hurt was gone.

Closing her eyes, she let Joshua tenderly carry her into the house.

Leaning against the pillows propped behind her, Laurel laughed at Kendra's imitation of the family throwing Jason Portland off of Catawba. The humiliation of her beating had finally diminished, and she was feeling better. She desperately wanted to see Joshua.

"So Joshua and Father hauled Jason to the end of the lane and threw him down like a dead fish," Kendra was saying. "And Reid, not to be outdone, told Jason that he'd thrash him soundly if he ever set foot on Catawba again." She giggled as she pantomimed her brother's fierce expression. Laurel finally interrupted her.

"Kendra, would you ask Father to allow me to go downstairs today?" she begged.

"I already did. He said you could sit in the parlor for a couple of hours if you felt up to it."

"Oh, thank you!" Laurel was surprised at her sister's thoughtfulness. "Can I go now?"

"Joshua is waiting outside the door to carry you down." Kendra grinned. "I didn't think you would mind him helping you. He's been skulking around in the hallways forever." Kendra and Laurel had spent a lot of time talking the past few days, and Laurel had told Kendra all about her love for Joshua. Kendra had been delighted.

"Did I hear someone say my name?" Joshua peeked around the door. Kendra smiled as Laurel went pink.

"Yes. Please come and get my complaining sister out of here. She's driving me crazy." Then, belying her words with a kiss to her sister's cheek, Kendra patted Joshua's arm and left the room.

Joshua stared after her thoughtfully. "She's too smart for her own good." He turned back to Laurel. With an arched brow and a smile, he lifted her into his arms.

Laurel felt a wonderful tingling sensation run from her toes to her neck as he carried her down the stairs. This man had saved her life. Even more wonderful, this man loved her. She snuggled closer, enjoying the feel of being in his arms.

"Be still, woman," Joshua grumbled softly. Laurel smiled.

The horrible ordeal was over. Jason was gone, and Clair had confessed to Taylor and Maida about the beatings. They had decided that she should stay with them a while longer. Everything was working out perfectly.

Joshua carried Laurel into the parlor and made sure she was comfortable on the sofa. She was surprised to see him suddenly go down on one knee beside her. Taking her hand in his, he cleared his throat and took a deep breath. "Laurel Marston, will you do me the honor of becoming my wife?"

"Yes. Oh, yes, Joshua." She pulled him up to her and he carefully wrapped his arms around her, grinning like an idiot. The next few minutes were spent renewing their love for each other.

"Well, good," Joshua said after a moment, pulling away from Laurel. If she noticed that his breathing was a little erratic, she didn't say anything. Likewise, he didn't mention that her cheeks were flushed and her eyes sparkled like gems. He set her back against the sofa and faced her.

"Laurel, there's something I want to do. I want to apologize for being such a cad these last few weeks." Laurel started to speak, but he held up his hand. "No, love, I want to do this." He paused and ran a hand through his hair, trying to think of how he could say what he had never told another soul before. Not even Matthew.

"I have treated you horribly, and for that I apologize. Actually, I've treated a lot of fine women horribly over the years. I did it because of my own anger, not because of anything they, or you," he smiled at her, "did. I did it because of something that happened to me a long time ago."

Laurel was silent, waiting. Joshua took a breath.

"You see, I was once very much in love with a very beautiful and proper lady. Her name was Grace. Grace Webster. She lived in Deerfield, New York. I was trapping at the time, coming in once a month or so to drop off my skins and pick up supplies. I ran into her at the mercantile. Literally ran into her." He stopped and looked at Laurel again. Her eyes were pained.

"You don't have to do this, Joshua," she whispered, taking his hand.

"No, I want to. I don't want there to be anything between us, sweetheart." He stood and walked over to the window. "Well, I was smitten right from the start. I started staying in town all the time; I cleaned myself up and got a room and courted her. She allowed my attentions and we often went out together for strolls and picnics or went to her house for dinner.

"She was very decorous, impeccably neat and tasteful, and insisted on proper manners and such. I was hardpressed to keep the correct gentlemanly attitude. At the time, I thought it was worth it. I did it for love of her.

"One day, I finally got up my nerve and kissed her. She slapped me." He paused and smiled at Laurel's faint gasp. "Yes, I had the same response. I told her that I thought it was perfectly acceptable, as we had been seeing each other for some time. Then I told her that I loved her and that I wished to ask for her hand in marriage. She turned me down.

"She told me that there was no way on earth she could ever marry someone like me—a trapper. 'What would people think?' she said. She had only been allowing my attentions because I was suitably attractive and because the other girls in town were jealous. It was," he grinned wryly, "quite a blow to my ego. I left town that night and never went back. I swore that nothing like that would ever happen to me again, that I would not allow the petty arrogance of some prim and proper woman ruin my life. I've had a bad attitude about women ever since."

Laurel held out her hand to Joshua and he returned to the couch to sit beside her. "I'm so sorry," she said, tears coming to her eyes. Joshua wiped them away.

"None of that. It's long over. And as you can see, I have gotten over it quite well." He planted a kiss on the bridge of her nose. "So, you can see why I had trouble with you from the start. My head was telling me to stay away from you, but my crazy heart wouldn't let me. Will you forgive the meanness of your betrothed?"

"Yes," said Laurel, leaning into his arms. "I don't care what happened before as long as we're together now." Then she pulled back. "There is one thing I would like to know, though."

"Anything, my love," said Joshua gallantly.

"What exactly happened to you in the swamp that day?" She laughed at the comical look that came over his face.

"You would bring that up again, wouldn't you?" he grimaced.

"I'm waiting."

"Ah, cruel woman. Already you rule my life."

"I'm still waiting." Laurel tried to keep from giggling as Joshua scowled down at her. With a sigh, he acquiesced.

"I fell," he muttered, not looking at her.

"You what?" She drew back in surprise.

"I fell. I had already checked my traps, and let me tell you, I had enough to win too." He smiled at her wickedly. "I was coming back fully prepared to take my reward. Unfortunately, I was so sure of myself that I didn't watch where I was going and fell flat into a pool of mud. I lost my animals, my traps, and my pride and had to come crawling into camp looking like a swamprat. I was quite humiliated." He looked at her with an aggrieved expression.

Laurel laughed at him, tugging him back into her arms. She couldn't wait to become the wife of this man. She had dreamed of a man who would love her for herself, and Joshua Douglas was definitely that man. She would make sure he was stuck with her for the rest of their lives.

Smiling wickedly, she lifted her face and lips to his. She was pleased when he took the hint.

As the end of October approached, Kendra became nervous. Court hadn't spoken a word to her since Pickle's death over a month ago. She'd tried catching him alone, but he continued to ignore her. Brokenhearted and discouraged, she was at the end of her rope. Today marked the end of his indentured service to Ward. Court was free to leave and never return. She had one last chance.

Clenching her fists, Kendra marched toward the barn. It was going to be settled right now. She wasn't going to let Court walk away without one more try. She was ready to tie him up and make him listen if need be. Her love deserved that.

The barn was empty, so she began to search the grounds. She knew Court was working close to the house somewhere. She finally found him splitting wood behind the farthest barn and halted, staring at his bare back.

Court's muscles bunched as he lifted the ax and let it fall. His back glistened with sweat. He attacked the wood with a vengeance, tossing each piece aside.

"Courtland Yardley, you are a coward and a rat," Kendra shouted.

Turning around, the ax poised in both hands, Court looked at Kendra coldly. "What are you doing here?"

"I should be with the man I love, but he keeps pushing me away and ignoring me."

Court turned and began splitting wood even harder. "Are you imagining that piece of wood to be my head, Court?"

"Yes," he growled.

"You can't get rid of me that easily."

Slamming the ax into the cutting block, Court whirled around again. "What do you want from me, Kendra?"

"Love," she said.

"No," Court refused.

Kendra stepped closer to him. "You still love me, Court. I know you do. If you leave Catawba after you're released tomorrow, I'll follow you."

"Don't you have any pride, Kendra? I'm not any good for you."

"I'll be the judge of that."

"You need someone who can take care of you and your children. I can't do that. When I leave here, I won't have anything but my clothes. I'll have to find work somewhere. What kind of life is that for a lady?"

"I don't care what kind of life we have. I want to be with you."

"No, Kendra. It won't work."

Kendra had been expecting this. Knowing how stubborn Court was, she had come up with one final solution to her problem. She knew that Court needed to feel that he could offer her something, that he could be her provider. He couldn't feel like that now when he was indentured and beholden to the Marstons. He couldn't even feel like that after he was released. He would have nothing. He needed time, she had realized. So she made her last gamble.

"Could we make a deal?" she offered.

That stopped Court. "What kind of deal?" he asked suspiciously.

"When you leave Catawba, I'll give you one year. If you can't find work and a home for us by the end of that year, I'll let you go without another word."

Court thought it over. He didn't know what the future held. He didn't even know if a year's time would make a difference. At least, he thought, it would give Kendra time to get over him.

"One year?"

"That's all I'm asking. I've waited for you over two years. I can wait another. Do we have a deal?" Holding her breath, Kendra held out her hand.

"You promise it's only for a year?" At Kendra's nod, he slowly reached out and shook her hand.

Kendra's face lit up with a smile. "I'm going to keep you to that promise, Court. I know you'll be back for me." Twirling around, she ran back to the house, her heart bursting with joy.

He said yes, she thought elatedly. *He said yes!* There was still hope for them, and that was all that she needed.

Courtland Yardley was set free the next day, and within the hour was heading toward Charleston with hopes of getting work. He was confident that the skills his father had taught him would be needed near the docks. But work didn't come and his hopes slowly dwindled. Weeks passed as he knocked on every door where barrels were made. One cooper after another turned him away.

Soon he had only one more place to try. The night before he was to go, he sat alone in his hotel room, thinking of Kendra. If he didn't find work here, he would have to leave the area and try elsewhere. He would have to give up hope of having Kendra before he'd even started. He stared up at the ceiling.

"Father God," he murmured. "You know what has been going on with Kendra and myself. You know how I have tried to give her up for her own sake. You know how she has given me this last chance.

"Lord, I need this job. I don't care what it is, I need it. It's my last chance for Kendra. I'm challenging you to give me this job. I have tried to be a godly man, but I need some help now. Help me, Father. Please." Court lay awake long into the night.

The next day, he stood outside the office of the manager in the largest company in the city. He wasn't very hopeful of getting a job. But, thinking of Kendra, he knocked anyway.

"Come in."

Opening the door, Court saw an older man sitting behind a desk, going over accounts. "What is it?" he barked, not bothering to look up.

"Excuse me, are you Mr. Morgan?"

"Yeah, what about it?" The gray-haired man finally looked up, taking Court in from head to toe.

"My name is Courtland Yardley, sir, and I was wondering if you had any positions for a cooper." Court nervously rolled the brim of his hat in his hands.

"We don't have anything now. Try back in a few months." Dismissing Court, the man turned back to his papers.

"Please, sir, I'll do anything. I need a job."

Mr. Morgan scowled as he returned his attention to Court. Court put every ounce of longing he had for Kendra into the look he gave him and the man blinked, his expression softening slightly. He sat back in his chair, giving Court an appraising glance.

"Yardley you say? And you've coopering experience?" Court nodded. "Yardley. Yardley?" His expression sharpened. "You ever heard of a Josiah Yardley from England? Any kin to you?"

Court's eyes widened in amazement. "Yes, sir. He was my father."

"You don't say? Well now, this is a coincidence. 'Was,' you say?"

"He passed away several years ago."

"I'm sorry to hear that, son." Mr. Morgan motioned for Court to have a seat. "Your father taught me everything he knew before paying my passage here to America. Bet you didn't know that. It was almost forty years ago. I never forgot him. He was a good man, Yardley was." He sat a moment, lost in thought. "Well, then. What brought you to this country?"

Court sat bemused. He could not believe that, of all people, he would meet an old friend of his father's. He allowed the smallest glimmer of hope into his heart. *Please, Lord.*

Pulling himself together, he explained what had happened to his father's business and how he had become an indentured servant to Ward Marston. "I'm looking for a job, sir. I can do anything and I don't mind hard work." He waited while Morgan stared at him thoughtfully. The man tapped his pen several times on the table, then nodded.

"Tell you what I'll do. I'm lookin' for someone to help me run the company. At my age, it's gettin' too difficult to get around. If you're as good as your father was, you'll be able to handle the job. What do you say to that, young Yardley?"

"I'm not sure I understand you, sir," Court said.

"You work for me for one year. In that time, I'll show you everything there is to know about the company. If, after the year is up, you want to stay on, I'll sign half of the business over to you and we'll become partners."

Court's jaw dropped. He stared at him blankly. "But, sir, isn't that something you should do with your son?"

"I never took the time to marry, boy. I don't have none. This gives me the opportunity to repay an old friend and get the best worker I'm sure to ever have. Are you up to it?"

Court agreed eagerly, scarcely believing his good fortune. He would start the next day. Returning to his small room, he dropped to his knees in thanksgiving. *Father God, forgive me for doubting you. You have taken care of me even when I wouldn't trust you. You are overwhelmingly gracious to your humble servant. Thank you!*

He couldn't wait to get word back to Kendra. She had promised to wait for one year. If he worked hard, he'd be able to get established in Charleston and build a home for her before that year was up. It was the least that she deserved and all that he desired.

Christmas had come and gone. In the new year of 1803, the Marston family had joyfully welcomed the birth of little

Allison Rose Marston. Kendra and Laurel now had another sister. She was beautiful, with rosy skin and dark hair like Maida's.

Sitting on the porch, a warm shawl wrapped around her shoulders, Kendra watched over Brooke and Daniel as they played. In the three months since Court's departure, she hadn't heard a word from him. She prayed for him every day, but it was becoming more difficult to keep her spirits up as the time slipped by.

Laurel was busily preparing for her wedding, which would take place in the spring. It was all she talked about now. Joshua was always at the house. Seeing their happiness only added to Kendra's pain.

Lost in her depression, Kendra didn't see the man who walked across the lawn toward her.

"Kendra."

Looking up sharply, she blinked several times before she could be sure she wasn't dreaming. "Court," she whispered. He smiled and she flew off the porch and into his arms. "Court, oh, Court, I've missed you terribly." She wept as she held him tightly and he showered hungry kisses over her face, whispering her name over and over. He couldn't get enough of her.

Finally, breathless, they pulled away to stare at each other. Kendra couldn't believe that he was actually there. She lifted a hand to his face and he held it there.

"I've come for you, Kendra."

Five soft words, yet they shot through Kendra's heart like lightning. Court had come for her at last. There would be no more waiting. She clung to him, knowing she would never have to let him go again.

Neither one of them noticed Taylor as she came out to the porch. She smiled at the scene before her. "Well, I guess this means that there will be a double wedding come spring."

Guiltily, Kendra and Court broke apart. They looked at her and then at each other. He hadn't even had the chance to ask her to marry him. Eyes twinkling, Court said, "Well, love?"

"You'd better believe it!" Whooping, he swept her up and twirled around and around the yard. Taylor only shook her head and left them to their joy as they collapsed in hysterical laughter on the ground.

All is well at Catawba, she thought.

Indeed, all was well at Catawba.

About the Author

Laurie Stahl, daughter of the late best selling author, Hilda Stahl, has begun working in her mother's footsteps. While assisting her mother with developing story lines and learning writing techniques, Laurie began to want to do her own work. Upon Hilda's death in 1993, Laurie's desire to become a writer deepened.

After two years of full-time ministry, Laurie and her husband, James, are pastors in Crystal River, Florida, with their two children, Seth, three, and Gabrielle, one.

Watch for the next book about the women of Catawba
coming in Winter 1996